Jacob's Path

Cries From the Earth, Book 3

BRENDA GATES

Copyright © 2023 Brenda Gates

All rights reserved. No part of this publication may be reproduced, distributed. or transmitted in any form or by any means, including photocopying, recording, or other electronic or mechanical methods, without the prior written permission of the author, except in the case of brief quotations embodied in critical reviews and certain other noncommercial uses permitted by copyright law.

ISBN: 978-1-7325602-4-6 (Paperback)
ISBN: 978-1-7325602-5-3 (ebook)

Any references to historical events, real people, or real places are used fictitiously. Names, characters, and places are products of the author's imagination.

www.brendagates.net

CHAPTER ONE

April 9, 1865
The War is Over
A flash of red.

JACOB Reddington felt the hair on the nape of his neck rise as he scanned the woods lining the road. After years where noticing small details could separate the living and the dead, he couldn't help himself.

He needed to relax. Lee had surrendered; the war was over. His side won. He glanced ahead at Johnny. Yes, they had survived. They were safe.

The arc of the sun was well on its westerly fall, and shadows cast about at odd angles as a breeze played among the leaves and branches overhead. The small party, seven in all, nudged their weary horses forward. If the road, which was little more than a well-worn path, remained clear, they would arrive in town within the half hour. There, a camp was set up with food and drink for man and beast alike. Tomorrow, after registering and turning over equipment to the proper authorities, a train would take them east. Take them home.

Ahead of him, Johnny laughed at some tale his companion was telling. Jacob smiled. He was bringing Johnny home, just like he promised. The war was over. They were going home.

With growing unease, Jacob once more looked over his shoulders, scanning the woods and the road. There was no one in sight. Had it been his imagination? A bird? No. Something lurked, barely perceptible: a heart beating at a different pace, a prolonged pause in the hum of insects, a hoof-beat other than their own.

Sunlight reflected off metal in a blink between branches.

"Get down!" He grasped the reins and threw himself off the side of his horse, pulling the mare between him and the trees. Johnny sprang from his mount a second behind Jacob. A shot rang out, knocking the lead rider from his horse. The rest leaped to the ground, scrounging for their carbines, rifles, shotguns—whatever they had tucked in the saddles.

Johnny's horse screamed and bolted forward as a bullet ripped through her abdomen. Johnny stumbled backward, blood gushing from his chest.

"Johnny!"

Chaos erupted, screams of men and horses mingled together. Jacob dropped to the ground, scrambling to Johnny's side. He felt a swoosh of air as another mount collapsed. Grasping his brother's collar, he pulled hard, desperately dragging him into the ditch and out of the line of fire.

Even with his uniform on, Johnny was too light. Wartime rations were never quite enough for the growing boy, despite Jacob sharing his own. Pulling him into a gaping hole in the moist black soil left by the rotting roots of a fallen tree, Jacob tore open Johnny's coat. A bullet ricocheted off a rock by his foot, and a stab of pain shot up his calf.

"I'm gonna die, Jacob."

"No, Johnny." Tearing off his jacket, Jacob stuffed it up against the gush of blood. His jacket slowly turned crimson.

Johnny grasped his brother's hand, eyes wide, face contorted. "What was—?"

Jacob put a finger to Johnny's lips. "Shh."

The shots paused. The air lay thick with gun smoke and silence, interrupted by intermittent moans. They hadn't had a chance. If only he had seen the ambush sooner.

A single shot pierced the air, followed by an eerie stillness that weighed heavy over the woods.

"Please!" A voice pleaded, broken by another shot.

Jacob peered around a clump of soil that clung to a handful of hair-like roots. A small band of mounted men observed the carnage from the forest edge, rifles at the ready. They wore no uniforms. It could be Bushwhackers. Maybe Confederates without uniforms. Perhaps local boys seeking vengeance.

One of their number, lanky and unshaven, a red ruffle lining his vest, sauntered from wounded man to fallen horse. A revolver in hand, he casually inspected each, shooting any that moaned or moved. There were six shots in all.

Two horses came galloping from the direction where Jacob's group had just come.

"All clear this way." The riders saluted the lone man standing amidst the slain.

"Good." The man tucked the revolver back in his holster and motioned to the rest of the gang in the woods. "Let's get ourselves something to drink."

Together, they galloped down the road toward town.

Jacob lifted his jacket to inspect Johnny's wound. The flow of blood was diminished. He covered it once more. His heart pounded with dread. Wounds like this were nothing new on the battlefield.

Johnny began shivering.

Jacob drew him closer. "They are gone. Hang in there, Johnny."

Long, almost delicate fingers held tight to Jacob's large, muscled hand.

"I am scared, Jacob."

"I got you, Johnny. I got you. You will be all right." It was a lie, and Jacob knew it.

"I done so many things."

"We all did. We had no choice."

"I didna want to." The anguish in Johnny's eyes tore at Jacob.

"I know. Me neither."

"The fire, Jake. There were children. I shoulda stopped him."

Jacob closed his eyes, picturing Captain Powers

walking out of the large farmhouse, fastening the top of his pants, spitting on the ground and smirking. His second in command, Sergeant Tanner, barricaded the front door looking smug. He was the one who reported the slave owner status of the people inside.

"Burn it." Powers directed the band of soldiers waiting outside. "Nothing inside worth saving."

"Sir?" Jacob had stepped forward. "Aren't there people inside?" He should have pushed harder. He should have checked the house himself. Instead, he tried to keep his brother from seeing what was happening. He hadn't succeeded.

"Was none of your doing," Jacob said, pulling Johnny closer, hoping his own warmth would ease the shivering. "You would have stopped him if you could."

"I didna even try." Johnny's hand was like ice. "I am going to hell, Jacob. I am gonna burn."

"No, Johnny. God knows. He knows you could do nothing to stop it. The guilt lies with them as gave the orders."

The boy smiled weakly. "Can God forgive me?"

"You are not to blame. I told you already."

The shadow of Johnny's first mustache twitched above his lip. "You been good to me, Jacob. Sorry I didna listen and stay home."

Jacob swallowed, tears trailing through the mud smeared on his cheeks. He buried his face in Johnny's thick red hair. It was his fault. God was punishing him for not trying harder. He had known. Deep down, he had known what Powers was doing.

"Tell Momma I am sorry. About leaving her. About the fire." Johnny clenched Jacob's hand tighter.

"I will not speak of the fire. You been brave, Johnny. Dang brave. I will tell her that."

Johnny's grasp on Jacob's fingers loosened.

"You are the best brother, ever." Johnny's lids drooped, then opened again. His pupils were large. He blinked as though struggling to focus, then coughed out a weak laugh. "Do not look so worried. It does not hurt so bad now."

"Good."

"Let me rest a bit. We'll talk when I wake."

"I am right here."

Johnny's breathing relaxed, small breaths that spaced further and further apart. Then nothing.

"I love you, Johnny. I love you, little brother." Anguish surged through Jacob's chest as he cradled Johnny's head, running his fingers through the boy's hair. A loud moan escaped his throat and he clung tight to the lean body, willing him to take one more breath.

"Oh, God!" he cried, rocking back and forth, gasping for air. "Please. Not him."

He remembered rocking Johnny when he was so small his head could rest in the crook of Jacob's elbow and his knees rested on the other arm. There were ten years between them, and Jacob always took care of his baby brother. Until now.

"You guard him with your life, Jacob," Momma wrote when she discovered her youngest son had run off to join his brother. "Do not bother to come home without him."

And Jacob promised.

Time passed. Darkness fell without a return of the gang who ambushed them. Still Jacob sat, curled up against the root of the tree, holding Johnny. He must have dozed, brought back to awareness by a light drizzle misting his face. The penetrating ache rose once more. He couldn't allow himself to think. Darkness of night pressed around him. A grave must be dug.

He'd dug many a grave over the past four years. A familiar numbness crept over him.

With his hands and a large stick, Jacob scooped out damp soil from the hole left by the uprooted tree. He worked through the fog that settled over his consciousness, without regard for his bleeding fingers.

Once the ground gaped large enough for his needs, he wrapped Johnny in the blood-stained jacket, placed the lanky, undernourished body into the depths, and piled dirt and rocks over the remains. Jacob formed a rough cross and propped it over the grave.

He should say something. A prayer, a verse from the Bible. Something. But his mind was empty, his lips without words.

He turned and stumbled up toward the road, toward the massacre of horses and fellow soldiers. He first found Martin. Always ready with a joke or a drink, he now lay staring at the heavens, shock across his motionless face, three bullets in the chest. Walter, from Jacob's hometown near St. Louis and father of three, had one leg under his horse, and a bullet in the head. Jacob turned away. They were all dead.

They had survived the war. It was over. But hell pursues the wicked.

He rifled through the packs with stiff, mechanical movements, looking for a canteen, a knife, a blanket. Night was on him. He would head on to the next town in the morning.

"Reddington."

A body protruded from beneath a large black horse, and a hand reached upward.

"Red. Help me." It was Captain Powers.

Uncomprehending, Jacob walked to where the captain lay.

He was dead. They were all dead. Maybe Jacob was dead too.

"Boy! Snap out of it."

Jacob blinked.

"Get this beast off of me."

Jacob tried to make sense of what he was hearing. Blood was everywhere. The Captain was covered with blood.

"You're dead, sir."

"That's the horse's blood, you idiot! Not mine. Get this animal off me."

"Yes, sir." He must be in a nightmare. It was time to wake up. How do you wake yourself from a nightmare? Grasping the captain under each arm, he pulled. Nothing budged.

Stepping back, Jacob inspected the horse, feeling like he was standing outside of himself and privy to someone else's reality. A good mare, he thought, his mind focusing on irrelevant details. Her protruding ribs would have filled in nicely with a few weeks of adequate feed.

Unwinding the rope from Powers's saddle, Jacob tied it around the horse's rear hooves. The other end he tossed over a sturdy limb overhead then wrapped it around the base of the tree. Looping the rope over his shoulder and across the width of his chest, he leaned into it. The horse's hindquarters inched upward. Jacob felt his muscles bulge with exertion and pulled harder. The beast rose farther.

Powers. Of all people to survive.

It would be simple to release his hold, crush the Captain, and leave. No one would know. Or care.

Jacob secured the rope and returned to Captain Powers. This time, when he pulled, the man slid from under the horse's weight.

One leg bent at an awkward angle. Pulling up Powers's trouser leg, Jacob grunted. A jagged edge of bone protruded below the knee. There was little blood. The same crushing weight that broke the leg had also stanched the bleeding. Jacob tied a tourniquet above the injury, in case the bleeding broke through.

"Your leg is broken, sir. I'm going to have to make a litter and drag you." *I got to wake up.*

Powers stared at his leg.

"It's not broken. I don't feel a thing."

A crush like that, a protruding bone, Powers should be screaming. Maybe he was dead after all.

"Sir, can you move your other leg?"

Powers's eyes narrowed as he focused on his foot. Nothing moved. Pushing with his arms, he tried to sit up, lifting his head and shoulder only slightly before falling back.

"Get me out of here, you fool, before they come back."

Jacob took his knife and went to the woods, returning with several long, straight branches and proceeded to make a litter. The captain's belligerent curses urging him to hurry slurred together in the background.

With Powers secured, Jacob turned to the others. His fellow soldiers. His friends.

He should bury them.

Instead, he dragged branches and covered them as best he could. Tomorrow. He would return tomorrow. He owed them that much.

Lifting the poles, he tucked one under each arm and dragged Powers behind him. One foot in front of the other.

The night air was chilled. It contrasted with the heat in his face and the burn of his hands. But it didn't matter.

A deep fog weighed heavy on him. His calf ached. He was so tired. Jacob looked at the road and forced himself forward. One step, then another.

A distant bullfrog added his mournful cry to the hushed hum of insects. A full moon lit the night, mocking him.

Just a few more miles. Then he could rest.

CHAPTER TWO

April 10, 1865
Ravings of a Dying Man

"WHAT KIND of idiots are you?" Captain Powers' voice pierced acrid air. Jacob eased his eyes open.

A small lantern burned from the tent pole overhead and rows of cots lined the walls. Gripping the edge of his own canvas cot, Jacob turned his head.

The Captain was on the next cot over.

No air moved. The stink of putrefied flesh made it difficult to breathe. Jacob hastened to sit up. Someone else needed this bed.

Nausea hit like a punch in the gut, and the tent started circling around him.

"Hey, soldier! Best lay back down," the medic called from Powers's side, motioning to Jacob to get his attention. "That shrapnel in your leg lost you a good bit o' blood getting here."

Jacob blinked, his head ringing.

"I need a real doctor," said Powers.

"Sir, he'll be back. He has others to tend to."

Jacob eased back, mindful now of soft sobs and occasional cries emanating from the surrounding shadows. This was real. He closed his eyes, trying to fall back into the numbness that had engulfed him during the night. He wished he would die.

"Don't move me, you fool. My spine is injured, or didn't they pass that on?" The captain's voice pierced the air.

Someone needed to hush the man.

"I need an x-ray, a neurologist! I need my lawyer!"

Must be fevered.

"Captain, I must take you to surgery. If that leg doesn't come off, you'll die." The medic sounded exhausted.

"Get away from me! You're not taking my leg! Get me the doctor!"

The medic hurried away. Jacob's nausea subsided, and the throbbing in his calf intensified.

If he breathed through his mouth, the stench wasn't as bad.

"Hey, you. Reddington. You awake?" the captain's voice rasped.

"Yes, sir." Jacob didn't open his eyes.

"You got to get me a real doctor, Red. Get me back home. They know what to do there."

Jacob didn't answer. Minutes passed. Someone from the other end of the tent called out for a bedpan.

"I can pay you," Powers said. "I got quite the stash. Help me out and I'll make you rich."

Silence. Jacob didn't want any part of the captain's wealth. He wanted to be left alone.

"Where I'm from, they have technology, man. They could make me walk again, they have drugs for the pain, and machines that can see into your body and tell exactly what's wrong with you."

Definitely fevered. Wounded men often ranted nonsense, but this was an unusual line of thought.

"I'm not from here. I got a family. I need to get home."

Jacob's stomach lurched. He'd had a family too. With Johnny gone, he could never go home.

"Here." Powers scrounged through his pocket and pulled out a folded leather purse. Reaching in, he removed a slip of paper about two inches wide and three inches tall.

"Here. Look at this. I haven't shown this to anyone since I've been here. Go ahead, take it. It's my family."

Grasping the proffered paper, Jacob held it up so the light reflected off its surface, then nearly dropped it. The images on the paper were so lifelike he could imagine them being real people in miniature, ready to walk out of the picture. And in full color! He'd never seen its like. Turning it over, he inspected it from all angles. It was magical, a painting from the greatest master painter in the world! And such fine painting—as smooth as a photograph but much more alive. It was also the most inappropriate painting he had ever seen.

A dark-haired woman with only her torso covered was standing on the sandy shore of the ocean, water swirling around her feet and holding hands with two identical little girls of about three. Her long hair blew unrestrained across her face. Laughing, her expression of pure joy reflected in the faces of her children.

"Who painted this?" Jacob held the paper at arm's length.

"It's a photo. I told you we have modern technology where I'm from." The captain's eyes burned with more than fever.

"Why would she be photographed with such little clothes?"

"That's her swimsuit. Things are different there."

Could they bring back the dead? "Not sure how I can help. Where you from?" Jacob asked.

"Two-thousand-two."

That was a lot of money. "No, sir, not how much you have. Where are you from? I cannot help if I do not know from whence you came, and with this kind of 'technology.'" He waved the picture in front of him. "I have never seen anything like it."

Captain Powers's voice dropped to a loud whisper. "That's what I'm trying to tell you. I'm not from here, I'm from the future. From the year two-thousand-two."

Jacob choked, a cough and a laugh trying to erupt simultaneously. He'd stood by fellow soldiers in the throes of death, witnessed them hallucinating, talking with people long gone, heard the toughest of them cry for their mothers, had even heard one confess to bank robbery. But of everything he had heard in this miserable war, this was the most ludicrous.

"Sir, the fever is getting you."

To his astonishment, Powers began to weep. Jacob closed his eyes. Sympathy was slow to come for the captain. This was a fitting way for a man like him to die.

But that photograph. Something about it mesmerized Jacob, something beyond its clarity and color. It was the beauty of a mother laughing and enthralled with her children. He lifted the photograph and gazed at it once more. Twins, little girls. This monster had a family, a wife and children that loved him. He had what Jacob always wanted, and he didn't deserve them. Without thinking, Jacob tucked the picture into his pocket and closed his eyes once more. Powers was rambling, Jacob wasn't listening. He didn't want to. His head hurt.

The doctor came by to check Jacob's leg.

"You took a good bit of shrapnel, young man. Mostly in the muscle. We were able to remove it all, so it should heal with no worse than a limp, barring infection. No sign of bone damage. You were lucky."

Lucky.

Jacob turned away.

"Now, you, Captain Powers." The doctor turned toward Jacob's companion and began removing the bandages. The reek of putrid flesh wafted from the wound. "That leg must be removed. Gangrene has set in, and it may already be too late."

Powers' pale face reddened. "Get your hands off me, you incompetent medieval quack! No one's taking nobody's leg!"

Jacob put his hand over the picture tucked in his pocket. If he had someone waiting, it might be worth living.

Despite the cries pressing in around Jacob, sleep overwhelmed him, and he dreamed.

Rushing headlong down a hill, he felt the press of fellow soldiers surrounding him. The soldier nearest him opened his mouth to call a charge when a cannonball fell from heaven, plowing through the open-mouthed soldier and the entire flank to Jacob's right. Jacob screamed at the men working the enemy cannon. He must stop them.

Bayonet raised, he flew. Musket balls were thick as rain, falling to his right and left, but nothing touched him. At last, he was on the enemy. Thrusting his bayonet through the unsuspecting soldier, Jacob felt the flesh give way. The man looked up, astonishment written across his face. It was Johnny. Johnny, holding the gaping hole in his chest.

"Why, Jacob? Why are you doing this?" Johnny pleaded, reaching out a blood-drenched palm in supplication.

Jacob awoke, gasping for breath, his shirt saturated in sweat. His heart pounded hard enough to bruise his ribs.

A drink and fresh air—he needed fresh air. He needed a distraction.

Around him, nothing had changed. Powers stared at the open door, mumbling under his breath. Deep patches of pink blotched his pale cheeks.

"Captain Powers?" Jacob said.

The captain stared straight ahead, lips moving.

"Roger." He'd heard it was the captain's name.

Powers looked up and attempted a smile. It was a pitiful, cracked smile that didn't reach the rest of his face.

"Red." The captain's eyes were swollen. "I knew you'd come. Help me. I don't feel my legs. If I could get some proper care, I'd be all right." He rubbed his eyes. "If I could just get home. Jacob, I'm going to die if I don't get home."

"Sir, tell me about home, about your family." Over the years, Jacob found that if he could get men to talk about their loved ones back home, it eased their torment.

Tears welled in the captain's eyes. "I been bad. So, so bad."

"Think about your girls. Tell me about them."

"Twins. Beautiful, perfect little girls." His chuckle rang of melancholy. "I never wanted to be a father, can you imagine that? Kids cry and whine, slow you down. My wife, she was all wrapped up in 'the children this and the children that.' Me? I became an afterthought, as far as she was concerned. It got better once they were in daycare." Powers rubbed his chin and sighed.

Jacob listened. Delirium was common in the hours before death.

After a long pause, Powers studied Jacob, then continued. "If only I'd known then what I know now. When it comes down to it, if a man doesn't have his family, he has nothing. I was a lousy father. If you ever have kids, be a good father. I been so bad. I need to go back and make it right. Reddington, take me home. I need to make things right." Powers began sobbing once more.

Jacob sat up on the side of his cot. His leg pulsed with pain, but there was no nausea this time. He set a hand on Powers's arm. Words always failed him in times like this.

"Tell me about your wife. Where did you meet?"

"Sofia. My wife is Sofia. She was a model for my company." Captain Powers smiled. "She was the most beautiful woman I ever saw. I took one look at her and knew she had to be mine. Not just beautiful, mind you. She was good. A good mother." His face darkened. "She's dead. Left me, left my babies."

Powers grasped Jacob's hand, his fingers cold claws digging into muscle, pulling him forward.

"Help me. I hid money in the chimney. The Whitmore's place out in Randolf County."

Another home they destroyed. A family thrown to the whims of war. They were one of the more fortunate. The only woman present was a grandmother, with three young boys in her care. Powers allowed her a change of clothes for each, a pack of food and a jar for water, then escorted them unharmed out into the open field before burning down their home.

"God will punish you all," old Mrs. Whitmore had shouted as the home built by her father shot up in flames.

A wave of nausea once more threatened to evacuate Jacob's already empty stomach. God *was* punishing them. Most of the men from their unit were dead. Was it wrong to hope he and the captain would die soon? Powers grasped his hand tighter, a wedge of wood locked in a vise.

"You can have it, along with the jewelry. You'll be set for life, just help me."

"No." Jacob shivered.

"Don't pretend you're innocent. You have the same blood on your hands."

"I want none of your money." Jacob jerked his hand away, breaking Powers's grip, and collapsed on the cot, wishing he was far, far from there. "For fear of God, man. That is blood money. We be damned enough already."

Captain Powers turned his head and spat. "That's war, boy. But then, you were always soft. You can help me, or you can rot here and die, like the rest of these people."

He was right. Jacob sighed, staring at the ceiling, blocking out the captain's intermittent curses. The man deserved to die. It was a pity he couldn't feel any pain.

They both deserved to die.

Jacob focused on the throbbing in his leg. Maybe it would get worse and the fever would take him. Better men were dead. Men whose people needed them, wanted them to come home.

Powers's curses slowed, eventually giving way to the slow, deep breathing of sleep.

Jacob's dream haunted him. He was the one who let Johnny stay. He was a fool to think he could protect him.

He tossed back and forth on his cot, unable to get comfortable. He didn't really want to get comfortable. Comfort eased into sleep. Sleep brought dreams, and as of late, those were not good.

Jacob watched as the doctor retreated from the tent, leaving a solitary medic to care for the rows of men. Moving from cot to cot, the medic gave a drink to one, the bedpan to another. Someone began retching. The stench of vomit and excrement became more intense. Jacob gagged. When the orderly passed by with the canister of water, Jacob waved him away. He pulled his blanket up over his nose. It smelled of horses and smoke. Better.

He looked with longing at the tent flap opening, wishing the wind would pick up. Outside, he could hear men calling out to each other, the clip of hooves, and the creak of wagons. The sun was high and the weather warming. Despite the temperature outside, Jacob was cold. Not a physical cold, but a hopeless chill to his very soul.

Why live? Not even God could forgive him.

"I'm cold," Powers called out as the medic passed by. The medic found another camp blanket and spread it over him. Still the captain shivered. His skin was gray, and the patches of red on his cheeks more intense. He coughed, a wet, phlegmy cough, took a drink from the canister, and coughed some more. His breathing rattled ever so slightly. Jacob remembered that rattling in so many of his fallen companions. They died, every one.

CHAPTER THREE

April 10, 1865
Mrs. Powers

J*ACOB DOZED*, and there she was again. Silky brown hair tucked behind her ears. She swayed, eyes closed, humming the now familiar melody. A tear escaped and trickled down the side of her face. He felt the ache in her heart, the loneliness. He wanted to wipe the tear from her cheek, wanted to hold her and ask who she'd lost to cause such pain. But as in every dream, she did not see him. The most he could do was hum along. She could hear when he sang, and his singing soothed her.

Jacob awoke to find a woman standing beside him. A bag hung from her shoulder, its contents weighing her down. In one hand she held a cane, while the other was clenched over her mouth as though to suppress a cry. She trembled like a deer frozen in the moment but with every muscle tense and ready to bolt.

"Ma'am?" Jacob half rose from his cot.

She looked familiar. Where had he seen her before? She was older, a few gray strands streaking her dark hair. A jagged scar ran from her temple to the side of her mouth, marring the perfect beauty she once had, but not removing it entirely. It came to Jacob like a heat wave. It was the woman from the photograph, the captain's dead wife. Her eyes were the same, except where in her younger self's image they had shone with pure joy, they now reflected a deep sorrow. A chill ran down Jacob's spine.

"What song was that?" Her voice was husky with emotion. She lowered her hand and stepped closer.

Jacob looked around, wondering what she was talking about. The fog of sleep lay heavy over him. Was he still dreaming? Could anyone else see her?

"Song? Ma'am?"

"You were humming. What song was that?"

"I'm sorry, I must have been asleep."

Mrs. Powers placed a hand on his shoulder, ever so light a touch, as though testing to see if he really was there. The weight of her hand, however light, was of flesh and blood, not a spirit.

"You were humming a song. Tell me, where did you learn it?"

She sang a few notes, the melody one now familiar to Jacob. His eyes widened. The melody from his dream.

"Where have you heard that song?" Her eyes shone as she searched his face.

"I do not know. It haunts my dreams some nights. I was not aware that I sang it out loud."

"Sofia?" Captain Powers's voice was tremulous, rising from behind Mrs. Powers. Her back stiffened, and she swallowed. Taking a deep breath as though to compose herself, she squeezed Jacob's hand and turned to face her husband.

"Hello, Roger." Her voice was deep, with an accent Jacob couldn't identify.

It was several moments before the captain responded. "Are you a ghost?"

"No. I'm alive."

"I thought you were dead." The captain's voice was barely a whisper.

"I'm here." She reached to touch the captain's forehead, almost as quickly pulling her hand back.

"I'm sorry." Captain Powers's voice trembled. "Sorry for what I did. Take me home. I'll treat you right, I promise. Just please, get me home."

"I can't do that, Roger. Wish I could."

A hard edge returned to the captain's voice. "Unless you can get me home, you're of no use to me." He coughed and spat on the floor, catching the hem of her dress. "Why are you here? Did you come to gloat, or to finish me off?"

Mrs. Powers was silent for a long while, her head bent. The fingers of the hand holding her cane grew white with the fierceness of her grip.

Just leave him. Jacob wanted to speak but held back.

"I knew the war was ending and figured this would be the area you would return to. I've been looking for you, Roger. I came to offer forgiveness."

Jacob closed his eyes, stunned, her words like a punch in the chest, knocking out his breath. Forgiveness. Why would anyone forgive Captain Powers?

"You should've died in those woods," he continued. "It hurts my eyes just to look at you." The captain turned his head away.

"That was your intent. But what you planned for evil, God intended for good. What you did," she reached a hand to her face, "changed my life. Roger, I-I found God."

Powers laughed, a coarse, scratchy sound. Not even staring death in the face changed this man.

"I found God?" He mimicked, turning back to face her. "You're no better than your mother. If it weren't for me, you'd be working the streets just like she did. *I'm* the one who changed your life. You worthless, ungrateful, lowlife."

"You're dying, Roger." Her voice trembled as she reached for his hand. "God stands on the other side. Are you ready?"

Jacob shivered. She spoke to the captain, but the words hit home. He was far from ready.

"Get out of here, Sofia. Religion doesn't suit you. Just leave."

"I'll be here, Roger, if you need me."

"I said leave. I have no wish to look at you."

Mrs. Powers stood motionless, her head bowed. With a sigh, she nodded as though in response to some hidden voice and turned to face Jacob.

Jacob shifted uneasily as she studied him, amused and unperturbed by his staring. When she smiled, a lopsided smile some would call grotesque, a strange sensation of peace flushed over him. There was something beautiful about her. It shone from inside, from beyond the scars.

Her eyes were as black as a moonless night, burning with concern and intelligence. "Tell me, why are you here?" she asked.

"Why would you forgive him?" Jacob burst with a sudden rush of anger. "That man, he is a monster."

She blinked. "It's true. But he's dying and in need. I am his wife. Sofia. Just call me Sofia." She sighed, glancing over her shoulder at the twisted form lying on the cot behind her. "I loved him once. I still do, but not the same way. But you, what is your name?"

"Jacob. Jacob Reddington, ma'am."

"And how do you know my husband?"

"He was the captain of our unit."

"I see." Her expression no longer carried with it the uncertain, vulnerable look she showed earlier. She looked sad. Resigned. "I'm a doctor. May I examine you?"

Without waiting for his response, she placed her hand on his forehead, then pulled a cone-shaped object from her bag and settled it on his chest. She bent low, placing her ear to the end of the cone. She had a clean scent, like the fresh air of a spring morning. As she listened, Jacob could feel his heart pounding a steady rhythm. It didn't matter how steady it beat. He was dead inside. Could she hear the death in him?

He watched her. He'd heard of women doing the work of doctors, but they were rare, and from the stories told by fellow soldiers, not very trustworthy. This woman oozed with professional confidence that was contagious. The anger that flared a moment before was gone, leaving him feeling like his head was in a haze.

"Are you injured?" she inquired once more, pressing her hands on his abdomen. He remembered his father, feeling the midsection of a sick calf, checking for swelling or unusual lumps beneath.

"My leg," Jacob said. "It is nothing. There are others worse off."

Pulling back the blanket, Sofia exposed Jacob's bandaged leg. With care, she unwrapped it, nodded, then wrapped it neatly once more. She pulled the blanket back over him and smiled.

"You're right. It could have been much worse. I'll have Thomas show you how to clean and dress those wounds, but I imagine you will heal quickly. Let's get you out of here, though, before you pick up an infection from one of the others. This place is a cesspool of bacteria."

Jacob raised his brows. She didn't rave like the captain, but she talked in ways unfamiliar.

That's what I'm trying to tell you. I'm not from here, I'm from the future. From the year two-thousand-two. The captain's voice echoed in Jacob's memory. No. The captain was fevered.

Yet, there was the photograph.

Jacob grasped the woman's wrist, gazing into her eyes as he reached into his pocket and pulled out the picture. "Ma'am, your husband—the captain. He gave me this. He said he wasn't from this time."

Sofia's eyes flickered with emotion as she reached for the photograph. Her hands shook ever so slightly.

"He wanted me to take him to his time. The future. You ever heard of such crazy talk?"

She swallowed, staring at the image in her hand.

"May I keep this?" When she looked up, Jacob saw shimmering and reflecting pools of light in her eyes, tears threatening to fall.

"It is yours, ma'am." A chill ran through Jacob's spine as he watched. She hadn't even blinked when he mentioned Captain Powers's outrageous claim. The photograph had not amazed her as it should have.

"Thank you." She hesitated, and then she smiled. Something in her expression soothed him. Opening her bag, she slipped the picture between the pages of a book inside. "We must talk, but not here. I will find you."

Voices outside the tent grew loud, and Sofia, giving his hand a quick squeeze, drew herself to her full height.

"What is going on that could not wait for me to finish my dinner?" The camp doctor stomped into the tent.

"Doctor." Sofia, head high, walked slowly toward him, extending her hand. "I asked for you and your men to come as quickly as possible. You have a cholera outbreak on your hands, and if this place isn't cleared out and cleaned immediately, these men will all die."

Dazed, Jacob watched as Sofia marched to the entrance of the tent, her limp barely visible. She appeared taller than before.

"What?" The doctor's face blazed red. "That is ridiculous. How could you—"

"Look about you, doctor. If you haven't picked up on the symptoms, you are more tired than you realize. Of course, if you and your men don't care to listen, I will have to report you to my friend Colonel Crittenden. He's already convinced the medical training in these parts is positively medieval."

Jacob smiled, his mood rising. It was as if hope suddenly permeated the very air in the tent.

The doctor paled. "Colonel Crittenden? You expect me to believe you are—friends?" His gaze coursed over her simple travel clothes, then lingered on her face. "You are not from these parts, not the kind of people the colonel socializes with. Are you his maid?"

Jacob cringed. He wasn't sure who Sofia really was, but she was not a maid.

"Actually, his wife, Carrie, and I are dearest friends, but Carrie does have the colonel's ear, and he trusts my judgment. I have the lady's letter of introduction, if you insist." She opened her bag, producing a well-worn paper.

The doctor opened the paper, glanced down at the signature, and coughed.

"My apologies, ma'am. I am unduly fatigued and welcome your assistance."

"Enough with the pleasantries. You there," she pointed to a large man glowering several feet behind the doctor, "start removing the patients from the tent. Try to find a sunny location for them. The sunshine will help burn off some of the bad humours. Keep the obviously sick apart from the rest. Dr. Easton is outside. He is with me and can direct you on what to do next."

"And you—" She pointed to another. "Have all the large pots you can find filled with water and place them over the fires. We need a lot of boiling water. The bandages and linen need a thorough cleaning. The men need to be bathed. Most importantly, and don't question me about this one, I want each of you to thoroughly wash your hands with soap and clean water between contact with each patient. Am I understood?"

The camp doctor lifted his brows and blinked repeatedly.

"Doctor?" Sofia planted her hands on her hips and stared at him. "We can't do this without your expertise. The colonel believes these techniques are saving lives, but we need to do them quickly. Do you understand?"

"Yes, ma'am."

"Oh, and this soldier—Mr. Reddington. He needs to be taken to Dr. Easton immediately."

Jacob watched in dazed silence as men hurried to their tasks unquestioning.

"Hey there, Red." A voice came from behind Jacob. Jacob tensed, twisting in his cot to see who spoke.

Sergeant Tanner, second in command to Captain Powers, stood by the Captain's cot, his eyes shifting from Powers to Jacob. Jacob's gut tightened.

"Sergeant Tanner, sir. You made it? When you didn't show at the rendezvous point, we all assumed you—" Jacob swallowed hard. If Tanner had joined the group at the appointed time, he might be dead as well. Why did good men die, and men like Tanner stood unharmed?

Jethro Tanner ran his hand through his grease-stained beard then spat on the ground. He nodded toward the cot where the captain lay motionless except for an occasional rattling cough.

"Fortunate for me, I wasn't with you. What of our captain there?"

"Gangrene. Refuses to let them take his leg."

"He alert?"

"Comes and goes."

Tanner grunted. "I been ordered to get you to the other doctor. Can you walk?"

"Yes, sir." Jacob reached for his knapsack.

"What you got there?" Tanner eyed the leather satchel, a vulture circling a carcass. "Never saw you with it. That belong to the captain?"

"No, sir. It is mine. Same as I've carried nigh four years."

"Humph." Tanner glanced around him. "Here. Let me help you."

Leaning on the man's shoulder, Jacob limped outside, breathing in the cool, fresh air. A few paces from one of the large pots of water now heating over the fire, he lowered himself onto a chair.

Jethro Tanner lingered, kicking a clump of grass with the toe of his boot.

"The captain, did he—you sure that is not his pack?" The sergeant hesitated, eyeing a tall, lean stranger hurrying toward them. "Aw, never mind. I best go get the captain outta there too."

"Hello, son." The man approached as Tanner hurried away. His brown hair was streaked with gray, his beard trimmed, and his once fine jacket was now threadbare but clean. He reached out his hand. "I am Dr. Easton."

"Jacob Reddington, of St. Louis, sir," Jacob sighed, returning the handshake.

"I believe you met my associate," he nodded toward the tent. A woman's voice, at once directing and soothing could be heard over the groans of the sick and grumbles of those rushing about. "You would know her as Mrs. Powers."

Their eyes met, and both men smiled. The doctor looked ten years younger when he smiled.

"Quite the lady, sir."

"The understatement of the year." Dr. Easton shook his head, grinning. "She never ceases to surprise me. So, did she pull the 'I have friends in high places' bit? She always seems to know what to say to get the troops moving."

He eyed a grouping of cots at the far end of camp and sighed. "It is too late for some of them. But I dare say, more will survive if we can get things cleaned up. I've been directed to get you cared for."

"Sir, I am fine. Others need you."

"Boss's orders." Dr. Easton grinned, nodding toward the tent. "Let me show you what to do with the wounds on your leg, son."

As Dr. Easton unwrapped Jacob's leg, he glanced up to look Jacob straight in the eyes. "Captain Powers, what did he do when she showed up?"

"I would rather not say."

The doctor stiffened.

"He harmed her?"

"No, sir, could not harm her if he wanted. He's dying."

Dr. Easton grunted. "Good."

Jacob arched one eyebrow. "'Tis an odd thing for a doctor to say."

The doctor's shoulders relaxed, and he gave Jacob an apologetic smile. Pulling a clean rag from his pack, he placed it in a tin and went to the pot of water now bubbling over the fire. He ladled some of the hot liquid over the rag and returned to Jacob's side.

Jacob watched nervously. If the doctor was thinking it good for one patient to die, what was to stop him from doing more damage to Jacob?

"You going to scald the wound, sir?" He shifted his weight in the chair.

The doctor laughed. "No, son. We'll give it a moment to cool off. The stream they're drawing water from is contaminated with the waste of all these men and animals and can make a wound fester. If you boil the water, it clears it of the contamination, makes it safe to clean the injuries, and to drink. The dirty water can kill you."

Jacob listened. It made sense. He'd noticed new camps rarely experienced illnesses that were prevalent among campsites long occupied. He preferred setting his tent on the outskirts, upstream from the rest, where the water was clear and not pissed in. But boiling the water?

He listened. Not that he cared, but he had been raised to show respect and to listen to those in authority.

Once Dr. Easton finished showing Jacob how to clean and dress his wounds, he left to tend to others.

Jacob rested on his cot, now on the perimeter of the lawn encompassing the field hospital. A tree gave sufficient shade without blocking the welcome warmth of the sun. If this had been any other day, Jacob would've been grateful.

A gentle breeze tugged at his hair. He ran a finger through it. He hadn't had the standard cut in a while, and as fast as his hair grew, it was almost long enough to tie at the nape of his neck. With his pack as a pillow, Jacob closed his eyes, letting the heaviness press him into sleep.

CHAPTER FOUR

Secret Codes

"*Tell me again.*" Sofia paced in front of Jacob, biting her lip as she walked. She and Dr. Easton had come to him shortly after breakfast. The captain had passed during the night, his rages renting the night until he no longer had breath to cry out.

Taking Jacob out of earshot from the other men, the doctors sat, talked, and pressed him to tell about his dream. Mrs. Powers cried when he spoke of the girl with the song, but never did she mock him. Instead, she began to teach him an odd sequence of numbers and pressed him to memorize what she taught.

Jacob looked up at the lady doctor, bleary eyed. He complied, despite the ache in his head, repeating back the series of numbers.

"Perfect," Dr. Easton said, nodding his approval.

Confused, Jacob recalled the morning events. There was something about Mrs. Powers that he found mighty peculiar, an air of confidence, authority even, not unlike her husband's. But where the captain's caused Jacob to be on edge, his wife brought with her a wave of stillness. Peace. Why had she picked Jacob, out of all the men in camp, to talk with?

Did she know he needed forgiveness as well? Could she be an angel like the captain initially claimed? She did have an otherworldliness about her. Jacob rubbed his forehead. That was crazy thinking. The captain's ramblings had gotten under his skin.

"Now you must practice that each morning and evening when you say your prayers. Think of it as a catechism of sorts." Sofia stopped pacing and lowered herself in front of him, leaning on her cane for support.

"Ma'am, it is rather strange, all you are asking me to remember. I don't understand. Is this some kind of spying you expect me to do? A code of some sort?"

"It is a code of a sort." Sofia placed a hand on Jacob's knee, "But no, I'm not asking you to spy on anyone. Ah! Who am I fooling?"

She turned her back and stared off into the distance. "You'll probably never need any of this."

Sofia resumed her pacing, her dark brows furrowed with thought. "It's just, it's just a feeling I have. That song. It means something."

She stopped pacing and sat beside Jacob. "The number is called what?"

"A telephone number," he said slowly. "Also referred to as a phone number."

"Yes. And who is it for?"

"Your brother, ma'am. And I'm to tell him I have a letter from you."

"Yes. It's very important you don't share that number until you need it. You will know when that opportunity arrives. When you place the call, you are to remain where you are. My brother will send someone to get you, he'll do whatever it takes to help. My brother is a good man, and, to borrow a phrase from a book I read with my girls, he's not always safe, but he is good."

He blinked. What on earth?

She smiled apologetically, "I've been missing for a long time, and he will suspect you. You may be pressed hard before he believes you are who you say you are. Do *not* share with him where I am. I will give what information I can in the letter. Don't elaborate. He won't believe you anyway. One more thing, never tell him *when* you're from—you'll understand what I mean."

Jacob nodded as if it made sense, despite her odd way of speaking and his lack of comprehension. Why hide where she was or where he was from? Her brother must be Confederate, and she didn't want him to find her.

Sofia handed him an envelope. "Chachi" was scrawled across the front. Strange name.

"This is for my brother. Keep it safe." She pulled a package from her bag. "And this is for you. Read it when you are well away from camp and have time to read in private. Within the pages of one, you will find what you are seeking for, Jacob Reddington. The other? Well, it is my own story. It will make little sense, but trust me. It's all true. Next we meet, you can give it back. I'll be interested in knowing what you thought."

Jacob reached for the package, curiosity rising through the fatigue. Sofia held on, searching his face, looking vulnerable, almost afraid. She bit her lip and let go.

"Please, guard them carefully. In the wrong hands, they could make trouble for me."

Sofia glanced over her shoulder and stood, smoothing her skirt. She coughed and positioned herself with her back toward the cots of sick men. "Jacob, Thomas, do either of you know that man standing at the entrance to the sick tent?"

Thomas shook his head. "No. He was helping get the men moved from the tent. I haven't had need to talk with him. He seemed healthy enough."

Jacob studied the man half hidden in shadows. "That is Sergeant Tanner. Jethro Tanner. He was your husband's man."

"I found him rifling through Roger's belongings this morning, and he has been shadowing me all day. He's also keeping a keen eye on you, Jacob. Any idea what he's after?"

"No, ma'am. He did ask if my knapsack was your husband's."

"Keep these away from him, please," she said, tapping the package she had given Jacob. "I don't trust him."

"Your instinct is correct, Mrs. Powers. Tanner is best avoided."

Thomas's brows drew together in a scowl. "Do not tell me we are free of one scoundrel only to have acquired another."

"It appears so." Sofia laid a hand on the doctor's arm. "Never mind. We will be more clever than he. From the looks of him, that won't be hard."

Jacob studied the man hiding in shadows. His mere appearance in camp was like the gathering of heavy clouds. An ominous presence. Jacob took a deep breath to shake off a mild sense of panic. He was being absurd. He had little respect for Jethro Tanner as a man, but they had fought side by side for the past three years. Each owed the other his life on more than one occasion. Tanner wouldn't give him any trouble.

Now, as for Mrs. Powers, that was another matter.

"Don't wander off unattended, ma'am. You will be safe as long as there are people for witness."

"We need to move on, Jacob." Dr. Easton tipped his hat and took Sofia's arm. He nodded toward the small cabin housing the secretary. "They are waiting for you in the office. The sooner you leave this camp, the better. The lady and I must be about our work. May God go with you."

It had been a long time since God went anywhere with Jacob.

Peace retreated with the departing couple. He lifted his knapsack, tucked Mrs. Powers's package inside, and slipped the strap over his shoulder. It contained everything he owned. Leaning on a crutch, he prepared to leave. Weariness engulfed him even as he forced his steps toward the cabin.

"Reddington. Jacob Reddington of St. Louis. I served under Captain Powers," Jacob notified the gentleman at the desk.

The secretary leafed through a pile of papers, pulled one out and glanced from it to Jacob. Without a word, he pulled two forms from a drawer, signed them, and slid them across the desktop.

"Here is a voucher for the past six months. At sixteen dollars per month, the total is ninety-six dollars for yourself." The secretary at last looked up from his books. Dark shadows circled his eyes. "And another for your brother. My condolences."

"Sir, if you could have both vouchers sent to our mother, I am sure she would appreciate that."

"I assumed you would be going home. Take it to her yourself."

Do not bother to come home without him. That's what his mother stated in her letter years before. Without Johnny, there was no place for Jacob to go.

Jacob shook his head, avoiding eye contact with the secretary. "No, sir. I will not be returning home."

CHAPTER FIVE

April 13, 1865

THE FAMILIAR cabin stood in front of him. Jacob shifted his weight from his good foot to the other, unsure why he had come this way. He had discarded the crutch miles before, it being more of a nuisance than a help. He would deal with the ache.

He was tired. Not just tired, but filled with weariness. This was unlike anything he had felt after battle. Unlike days of walking through mud that sucked the boots off his feet. Unlike the fatigue of going days with half rations.

This was a weariness that came from knowing you lived when better men lay dead in the cold ground; an apathy that came from the desire to lie with them. It was the weariness of being afraid to sleep because those better men haunted your dreams; a bone-deep lethargy because what little sleep you gave in to was broken by sudden terror at any sound emanating from the night.

It was the heaviness that came from fearing death yet longing for its embrace. It was the weariness of fearing the nightmares, yet longing for sleep, because only then did he dream of her. She, whoever she was, was the only salve to his broken soul.

He had no place to go. Belonged nowhere. Nothing good was left but the dream of *her*. The dark-haired stranger. She kept him walking. One foot, then the next. Two days of walking, stopping only long enough to rest his aching leg, to eat and drink. An hour of sleep here and there.

Now he stood at the steps of Aunt Catherine's cabin, wondering why he had come.

A curtain fluttered, and Jacob's stomach tightened.

"It may be best if I leave now," he muttered to himself, turning to go, "before she sees it is me."

The cabin door opened.

"Jacob Reddington? Jakie? Lord have mercy! Is that you?"

Jacob halted and turned back toward the house.

Aunt Catherine rushed toward him, arms outspread. She was thinner than he remembered, and her once bright red hair was now dull and streaked with white. She engulfed him in a hug.

"Jakie!" Tears streamed down her cheeks as she reached up to grasp his face between her hands. "My boy! Is it really you? Thank God!"

Her embrace awakened memories from a life Jacob had all but forgotten. He wrapped his arms around the little woman who had been the rock for his family after his father's death. He could feel her ribs through the threadbare fabric of her dress. The frail frame where once had been strength burned through to the empty place that was his heart. Jacob buried his face in her hair, breathing in her scent.

"Auntie," his voice broke, "I am so sorry."

"Now, Jakie boy. None of that." Aunt Catherine pulled back, wiping a hand across her cheek. Her eyes shone, a reflection of her smile. He loved her smile. It was so much like his father's. "You are here. For today, that is enough. Come inside. You look like you haven't eaten in a month of Sundays."

"I am not very hungry."

"That is the most hair-brained thing you could say. Look at you, boy, nearly as worn as those trousers you be wearing. Methinks you need a good meal and a bath."

A touch of a smile pulled at the corner of Jacob's mouth. He could never put his finger on what it was about Aunt Catherine. It was as though her spirit oozed out and infected everyone she touched. He could feel those fingers of life reach out and arouse his dying soul, tendrils of hope inching into the fog that pressed him down. He took her extended hand and let her lead him inside.

The house was as he remembered, but different. Spotless, checkered curtains pulled back to let in the full light of day and the fresh breeze laden with the scent of springtime. The wide, hand-hewn pine table sat below the window, right where it always had. Four chairs tucked in where once there had been eight. The fireplace held the same large iron pot that so often fed a houseful of guests. Their only child having died in infancy, Aunt Catherine and Uncle George had purposed their lives into caring for those around them who needed help.

The gold-framed mirror was gone, as well as the grandfather clock Uncle George treasured. The wall that once housed the piano stood barren, the Persian rug from the center of the room had been replaced by a colorful rag rug.

Aunt Catherine nodded at the empty space where the piano once stood. "I was very thankful for our earthly treasures. Seems there were still folk out there willing to pay good money for some of those old luxuries. It kept food on the table, young man. Seein' as I could not eat mirrors or pianofortes, I'm thankful I got enough cash to keep us fed."

"But Uncle's clock—"

"He'd a been proud to provide for me even in death." A muscle twitched in her cheek. Selling the clock had been hard, Jacob could tell. Probably harder than selling her beloved pianoforte. Uncle possessed little that he loved, and that clock had been his pride.

Jacob swallowed. He knew she was right. Uncle would want Catherine taken care of, no matter what the cost. What had Jacob's mother been forced to give up during the past years? He and Johnny sent her every spare dime from their pay. Had it been enough? Had she received Johnny's final check? He must not let his mind go there.

"Johnny is gone."

Aunt Catherine sucked in a deep breath, hand frozen as she leaned over the iron pot, bowl in one hand, ladle in the other. Her hand trembled, then she reached down and scooped out the thick stew and filled the bowl. She stood, her back to him. He could see her chest rise and fall as she breathed in deep, see the muscles in her neck tighten as she swallowed. Her shoulders straightened, and she turned to face Jacob. Tears glistened in her eyes.

"I am so sorry." She did not scold him, didn't point out how he had failed, how he should never have allowed Johnny to stay in the army. When he looked into her eyes, they held no accusation. They held nothing but love and a shared grief.

Placing the bowl on the table, she opened her arms to her nephew. A tear ran down her cheek. He ran to her, letting her hold him and sway with him back and forth, like she had when he was a child crying over the loss of his father.

And for the first time, Jacob wept.

CHAPTER SIX

Insisting she would not have him foul up the linen, Aunt Catherine chased Jacob outside to the pump house with instructions to use the soap on clothes and body alike, then to put on the clothes she'd collected from his uncle's belongings. The cold water was invigorating. Jacob found the smoothness of his Uncle's clothes comforting.

Once clean, he presented himself to his aunt as he had as a young child many years before, awaiting her approval.

"You clean up nicely." She nodded and smiled, then beckoned for him to follow.

"I gave Ellen and the child the big room." Aunt Catherine strode up the stairs with Jacob trailing behind. "I have spare quilts and pillows in the attic."

"The east room is more to my liking," she went on, "seeing as I am but one person and it is plenty big for me. It allows me to witness the sunrise of a morning. I always did say we needed a bigger house, but your Uncle claimed we had a spare room for lady guests, and men would be content staying by the hearth." Aunt

Catherine gave Jacob an apologetic smile. "I hope you don't mind. It will be nice to have more company in this empty home."

"'Tis a luxury after sleeping on the ground. Who is Ellen?"

"Yes, Ellen." Aunt Catherine paused, giving her nephew an appraising look and grinned. "She is quite the dear, off visiting her husband's folk this past week, they wanting to see her child. Ellen's husband was killed in the war, you know, she a widow these past three years. She and I been helping each other, but she can use a man. My old bones do not take to gardening like they once did, and we'd not have fared so well had Ellen not taken the bulk of that burden. She would make a fine wife for a man as was looking."

"So, her family would not take her in?" Jacob was not a man who was looking, for a fine wife or otherwise. Besides, if Ellen was living with his aunt, she was likely a charity case.

Aunt Catherine gave Jacob a sideways smile. "Ellen is from Charlestown. Her folks owned a plantation there afore the war. Gave it all up, she did. The fine home, servants and all, to marry. Her husband's folks never accepted that their boy married a Confederate, though she is as true a Union woman as they come."

"Yet she takes the child to visit his family?"

The firm line of Aunt Catherine's mouth and curt nod spoke volumes.

"They are his kin, she says, and have the right. As I said, she is quite the dear. No doubt when she returns tomorrow, she will attack the garden with a fervor that would drive Beelzebub away in fright. She says working the land soothes the soul."

His leg ached by the time they reached the top landing, but Jacob stood patiently as his Aunt piled his arms full of quilts and pillows.

"'Tis spring, Auntie, not the depths of a Canadian winter."

"I want you to be comfortable, and I have quilts in abundance. Had I been a better hand with the stitching, I might have sold those off as well. Guess the Lord knew guests would need a bit of unadorned warmth."

Handing Jacob the lantern, Catherine placed a hand on his arm. "Morning comes early, and I must rest. Do say if you require anything else."

Moments later, Jacob found himself on the floor atop a layer of quilts. Turning from one side to the next, he couldn't get comfortable. Pushing up on his elbows, he dragged his knapsack to him, lifted the flap and pulled out the leather-wrapped package. All the time walking here, he could not bring himself to open it. It was time.

The tie slipped easily apart, and the oiled leather wrap fell open. Curious, Jacob sat up, pulling the contents onto his lap. Two books sat one atop the other.

Within the pages of one, you will find what you are seeking, Jacob Reddington. The other? Well, it shares my own story. It will make little sense, but trust me. It's all true.

He opened the bigger of the two and recognized its contents immediately.

Holy Bible.

Sofia was written on the first line of the page where family information was documented.. Black ink covered where once a surname had been and over the black was a phrase written in tiny, neat script, "Now therefore ye are no more strangers and foreigners, but fellow citizens with the saints, and the household of God."

That was odd. Maybe she didn't like her connection with the captain. He didn't blame her. His eye scrolled down the page to the lines for births and marriages. The marriage line was blank. The birth date made Jacob's brows rise. The woman must have been very tired when she wrote there.

Birth: September 27, 1974

As he turned the page, a loose paper slipped out and into his hand. Jacob saw his name at the top in the same small handwriting.

Jacob Reddington, the pages of this book have saved my life. It is the most precious thing I own. Contained within its pages you will find underlined the verses that meant so much to me, along with my personal thoughts penned in the margin. When I wrote those, I had no intention of ever sharing their contents with anyone. I see you are torn with guilt, as was I not so long ago. You believe God can't forgive you. I believed the same because of things I had done. We both carry the weight of innocent blood. In these pages, you will find that God indeed will forgive you, and more than that. He will make of you a new person. He loves me, and He loves you, despite our many faults. Our God extends to you His grace. He already paid for our sins.

Sofia J.

Opening the book to the page marked with a silk ribbon, Jacob could see what Sofia meant. The first chapter of Ephesians, verse seven was underlined, a star marking the border beside it. "We have redemption through his blood, the forgiveness of sins, according to the riches of his grace."

Jacob slammed the book shut. That was all fine and dandy, but Sofia had no idea what he had done. He picked up the second book, opened it to the first page. Mrs. Powers's script was neat but so small it was as though she was afraid for her writing to be seen.

Journal Entry

October 30, 1853

At least she got her dates in the right century.

This is not my life. I am a mother with two beautiful girls, and my babies need me. I beg God every day to let me return. But God does not listen. Their faces follow me everywhere I go, always just behind my eyes in the background of what currently is.

While in Missouri, I would go daily to the springs where I came through. I sat and stared into the stillness of the water. Hoping. Waiting. Watching.

I am still here.

Now I've found a new place to sit and wait alongside a small creek bed behind my temporary home. Hidden amidst the forest, there's a spot that maintains a steady pool of water, even though most of the creek bed is naught but mud. I wonder if it is fed by some small spring. If the animal prints mean anything, wild creatures also frequent this location. They are either nocturnal, or they avoid my company, as I have yet to glimpse them. Maybe it's for the best, seeing that some prints are quite large.

I'm in Arkansas now, where Papi's people came from, and I search for him. Maybe he will know how this works and how I can get home. But who am I kidding? If he figured it out, he would have come back to us. To me. To Chachi. Most of all, to Mama.

Amadahy says she knows of no one who has returned.

With Dr. Easton's help, I've sent messages to each church registered in the state of Arkansas, asking for help in locating Papi. He would never miss a Sunday worship. Surely one of these messages will find him.

Journal entry

October 31, 1853

Mrs. Easton says I will find the answers to all my questions in the Bible. Tia Lupe used to tell us the Bible was a book full of mystery, and God revealed the answers to those seeking to learn.

Why am I here? The age-old question. I have more reasons than most to ask it. I need to know, so I will read. Sometimes I find peace in what I read. Other times, more questions.

Last night I read until my candle ran out of wick. My first reaction was to turn over and flip the light switch. Instead, I lay in the darkness staring at the ceiling. I never realized how limited the night is without electricity.

Movies. I miss sitting down and watching a good show. Then there's the music. Being able to sit in my chair with headphones on, and feeling like I sat in the middle of a symphony orchestra, or hearing a song sung as though it was all for me. All at a push of a button, or the turn of a knob.

Everything is so quiet here, except in the evenings when Mrs. Easton sits at the piano and plays. She could play in Carnegie hall and fit right in, that's how good she is.

The music reminds me of my girls, so I sit and listen and try not to cry.

She likes singing hymns. That woman is full of more religion than anyone has a right to be. But when she's singing, I don't mind. She quotes scripture verses all the time, not like the nuns at the girls' school, but in a manner that doesn't rankle. It comes naturally, like it's part of her normal speech, and while I will never admit it to her, I do find it reassuring.

"For thou, Lord, hast made me glad through thy work: I will triumph in the works of thy hands," was Mrs. Easton's verse for today, all the while sweating over steaming hot water with lye soap eating at her hands and scrubbing away at her son's blood-stained apron. I helped and hated every moment.

As I scrubbed, I couldn't help but notice my hands. I remember having my nails manicured and polished every week. Beautiful hands were important to me. It seems so silly, but I hate seeing my hands get all dried and cracked. I will set about trying to find a cream or oil to protect my skin. I may have to work hard for a living, but there's no need to let myself fall apart. My looks are all I have left.

Despair plagues me and I fight it, sometimes with success, sometimes not. I keep reminding myself that I started off life penniless, with nothing but determination and the beauty I inherited from my mother. I made it big in my past life. Here I am again. Penniless. No useful skills. Of value to no one. Without a husband. Without my children. I don't even have Chachi to watch over me. I am alone. Now, I must find an honest way to make a living. I have to succeed in this time and place. What choice do I have? I must survive. For my children's sake, I can't give up.

Jacob gently closed the pages, his eyes heavy. So much of what she said was nonsensical. Was this the same woman he met at the hospital? He could never imagine that Mrs. Powers struggled so much with a sense of worthlessness. He recalled the way she carried herself, her confidence, her gentle but powerful presence. He remembered her face and wondered what happened. Even with the scar, her inner beauty shone through. What changed her?

I came to offer forgiveness.

He leaned back, feeling the poof of air release as the pillow cradled his head, and he closed his eyes.

CHAPTER SEVEN

From the Future?

D*AYS PASSED*, one melding into the next. Aunt Catherine, ever the believer in work helping the soul, found plenty for Jacob to do. She tolerated short breaks to relieve the ache in his leg but had little patience for his self-pity. When not cutting wood or repairing the structures about the property, he helped by clearing more land for the garden.

Ellen proved a capable woman, every bit what his aunt described. She rose with the dawn to work the garden before the heat grew strong, then returned to tend to her daughter, Ruthie.

Her delicate features had been edged and toughened by years of hard work and limited food. Clear blue eyes shone with intelligence and a wit that could be either kind or sharp, depending on the conversation.

Ellen mothered her little girl with tender, yet firm patience, giving the young child tasks that challenged her. The war had forced them to rely on each other and work to the limits of their abilities.

Jacob wished he could take on the weight of Ellen's responsibilities. Still, every time he looked her way, it was the image of a darker, mysterious girl who haunted his thoughts.

Aunt Catherine was right. Ellen needed a husband, but Jacob was not that man.

Ruthie was a delightful little girl, coming to him unafraid and full of questions. She would find him where he wandered and take his hand, asking questions: why do some animals dig dens and others build nests? Why did the tree bear only apples when she wanted pears as well? Why? Why? Her vocabulary astounded him, clear and concise despite her small child's voice. And the endless questions! Sometimes Jacob thought the women sent the child to him because they tired of forming answers.

"How old are you?" he asked once.

"I will be five this fall. Mother says I am five going on twenty. How much is twenty?"

Evenings were spent in companionable silence, Jacob reading while his aunt mended clothing.

Whenever he rested, he read, sometimes from the Bible, sometimes from the doctor's journal.

He read and reread the passage where she described breathing life back into a child brought to her already dead. She claimed he still lived, but that his heart and breath had stopped. If that wasn't the same as dead, Jacob didn't know what it was. If he had brought Johnny to her instead of burying him by the tree, could she have brought Johnny back as well?

She described this CPR she performed, claiming it was something any person could do. That it was all science, and not a miracle. He doubted what she said.

He had sensed a power in her when she tended to him. Something of the Spirit of God. His admiration for the woman rose, and he read on.

He read of how she shied from caring for a man with a gunshot in the leg. She had changed much from that date till the end of the war. The woman he met didn't shy from the worst of the sick.

Reading late into the night helped distract him from memories he wished to avoid, and so he read until no longer able to keep awake.

Restlessness roamed through his bones. This wasn't home. He had no home. He should move on, but something kept him from leaving.

* * *

Journal entry

November 1, 1853

Memories flooded back as I opened today's paper. Anger abounds between the two parties, one desiring that Kansas remain free of slaves, the other demanding they have the right. In six months' time the matter will be settled in what will be known as the "Kansas Nebraska Act." Many slave owners in Missouri will flood over the borders, and the border war that begins there will push us toward the Great Civil War.

I remember Roger and I visiting Civil War museums, dragging our little girls along. His passion for the history and battles of the region pressed us onward, go, go, go, while drilling the girls on dates and facts until they could recite them back like parrots in a cage. How they hated it. Those were the "good" memories.

I remember lying on the floor with Roger kicking me, both fear and rage burning hotter than the pain, wondering if I would live to plot my revenge. I remember standing knee deep in the springs, seeing Papi's face and then falling through the frightening abyss of time.

My desperation to get to my girls remains as fresh as if someone had slapped me in the face moments ago. Now I am here, and Roger has our babies. He was always bigger, stronger, smarter. Luckier.

I was born on September 27, 1974. I know what is going to happen. One would think being from the future would leave me with a distinct advantage. But it does me no good. What good is knowledge when I can tell no one for fear of being seen as a witch or a lunatic? No one would believe me anyway.

Jacob stared at the page, rubbed his chin, then rubbed his forehead. He closed his eyes, opened them again. The words were still there. From the future. Jacob laughed out loud and slammed the book shut.

"What is so humorous?" Aunt Catherine looked up from her stitching. The oil lamp sat on the small table between them so they could both see in the evening darkness.

As was their habit, Ellen and Ruthie had retired to their room after the evening chores, leaving Jacob and his aunt to spend the quiet hours together.

"This journal. I believed Mrs. Powers was as sane as any, but Lord have mercy, she is a lunatic!"

"The lady doctor you told me about? The one who gave you the Bible and said it had what you were looking for?"

"Yes, the same."

"She was correct about the Holy Book. What leads you to conclude she is insane?"

"She says, see, right here, she says, let me read her own words—*I was born on September 27, 1974. I know what is going to happen. But it does me no good. What good is knowledge when I can tell no one for fear of being seen as a witch or a lunatic? No one would believe me anyway.*"

Aunt Catherine's brows went up. She brought the fabric to her mouth and bit off a thread. "That would lead one to question her sanity indeed. Did she write anything else you find odd?"

"Throughout the entire journal she uses strange words and references that make no sense, at least not to me. I assumed it was because she was a physician and knew about things I had not heard of. Look here, just before she wrote the statement I read to you, she predicted the passing of the Kansas Bill, although she refers to it as the Kansas-Nebraska Act. She also rightly predicts how this bill influences the start of the War Between the States–which she refers to as 'the Great Civil War.' All happened as she predicted." Jacob shook his head. "Bah! She must have written this after the fact and fudged on the dates."

"Perhaps she had a word from the Lord."

Jacob raised one brow and pursed his lips, his mustache twitching. "From the future?"

"Well, there is that." After a moment, Aunt Catherine chuckled. "She's right, though. What good would it do her to know the future? No one would believe her."

Jacob half grinned but didn't share her humor. It made no sense, and that bothered him.

They sat in silence, Jacob staring into the steady flame of the oil lamp.

Foreknowledge would be helpful in battle. Captain Powers had an uncanny ability to tell where a battle would occur and what location would put his troops to greatest advantage. He also claimed to be from the future...

No. That was insanity.

What about the photograph? No. Still not possible.

What if it is true? A voice whispered. Jacob startled, glanced about the room. Windows remained closed against the still cool nights. His aunt sat in her chair, leaning over her work.

"Impossible." he answered.

Aunt Catherine startled, nearly poking her lip with the needle. "What?"

"I said it is impossible." Jacob gripped his hands together, knuckles turning white.

His aunt looked puzzled.

"You asked, 'What if it is true?'" Jacob responded to her unvoiced question.

"I said nothing."

"But—"

She looked at him with brows arched. "You been hearing things?"

He had. He had heard a voice. Clear and succinct as someone speaking in his ear. God? He shook his head. It couldn't be. He could believe in God, but God didn't speak out loud, and God definitely wouldn't support someone's claims to be from the future. No. He, Jacob Reddington, was as crazy as the doctor.

I remove mountains, and they know it not. I shake the earth out of its place, I command the sun and it does not rise, I seal up the stars. What is time to me?

He was imagining things, voices repeating verses he'd read this morning in the book of Job. With a bit added.

His aunt returned to her work in silent concentration.

Jacob moaned. Just when he was getting better, feeling like life had purpose and hope, he began hearing voices. He was more broken than he had imagined.

CHAPTER EIGHT

Ghost From the Future

Journal Entry

June 1858

I felt him before I saw him, in that mysterious way people can tell when someone is staring at them with unusual intensity. As he moved toward me, I returned his gaze. A shiver ran down my spine. It was a vision. A dream. A ghost from my future. My past. I blinked, then stiffened, recognition flooding my senses. What fate had him follow me to this time?

Coming to a halt at the bar in front of me, he smiled. It was that perfect face. The one that won my heart so many years ago. Impeccably groomed, even white teeth, perfect complexion. Eyes my favorite hue of blue.

I stared, unable to speak.

"Hello, Sofia." His voice was as I remembered. A voice made for radio, or television. All of him was made for television. If you could call a man beautiful, Roger would be that man. Looking at him, even after all these years, made my heart flutter. He had aged a bit, but he looked so good. Was he the same man I knew, or had time gentled him? I wanted to throw myself into his arms, but uncertainty held me back.

I was right to fear him.

His hand shot out, like the uncoiling of a snake. Grasping my wrist he yanked me toward him, jealous and possessive as before.

I knew then that my chance at happiness is non-existent. He will force me to go with him. I can fight, but Roger always gets what he wants. My mind flooded with pictures of Edwina, locked away in a cage in that dreadful asylum. Roger will do that, if I don't cooperate. Would that fate be better than returning to this man who claims me?

It was when Thomas tried to step in that I knew the true price my freedom would cost. If I refused him, Roger would see Thomas dead. My freedom isn't worth it.

"Jacob?" A child's voice startled Jacob from his thoughts. "Yes?" He jumped, twisting to face Ruthie.

A finger twisted a strand of pale yellow hair that hung loose over her shoulders and her freckled nose scrunched up in a questioning look. "Are you lost, Mr. Jacob? I tried calling you and you do not answer."

"Lost?" If she knew how lost he felt, she wouldn't ask.

"Yes, lost. Mama says you get lost in thought, and that is why you do not answer. I thought you were being rude, but Mama thinks otherwise. Were you lost?"

"Indeed." Jacob smiled, allowing Ruthie to help pull him to his feet. "I am lost."

"Well, since I found you, I am to tell you to come eat." She took his hand and grinned up at him. "The book makes you lost? You become deaf each time you read it."

"Good books will do that. It is like slipping away to a different place, a different time." He wanted to tell her he was lost long before reading the book.

Ruthie nodded. "Yes, I see how that can be. When Mama reads to me, sometimes it is as if I am part of the story. I will like to read for myself someday. Then I will get lost sitting beneath a tree, and when Mama calls, she will know I am not being rude by not answering. It is because of the book."

Jacob chuckled. "It would be wise to keep your ears open. If I did not come when called, my mother would not let me eat."

Ruthie's eyes grew wide, her mouth forming a perfect O. "That would be dreadful. I hate to miss a meal. We missed so many during the war that sometimes my stomach would ache all night. I hope that never happens again. Let us hurry. I hope we are not too late to eat."

Jacob let her pull him up the steps, across the porch, and into the house where the aroma of fresh baked bread filled the air. Aunt Catherine and Ellen sat at the table. Each looked up with a welcoming smile as the two entered. The meal was simple, consisting of bread and beans. Jacob knew the larder was almost empty, and he chastised himself for not seeing to this sooner. Tomorrow he would go hunting.

He noticed Sofia's Bible still on the corner of the table where he had left it this morning. He'd meant to take it with him but took the journal instead.

Sofia found the answers she was looking for in those pages.

Jacob sat and slid the Bible from the table to his lap. He would take it in his pack while hunting and continue to search its pages.

* * *

For two nights and days, Jacob wandered the woods, rifle strapped to his back, setting traps and hunting game, a mare borrowed from a neighbor in tow. For hours he sat, silently rubbing his sore calf, waiting, reading.

The stories were familiar; Jesus, born of a virgin, in a place where sheep were birthed and fed. There was the story of Jesus feeding the five thousand, healing the leper and the blind. Even the story of Jesus raising the dead.

Some stories took on new meaning.

Jacob wept reading the story of Lazarus. He repeated the verse out loud. "Then Martha said unto Jesus, "Lord, if thou hadst been here, my brother had not died."

He let his eyes search the blue sky peeking through the trees. "God, if You had been there, Johnny would not have died. Where were You?"

He slept little, watching through the night, and it paid off. By the time he was ready to limp home, the borrowed horse was loaded with two deer, several turkeys, and a half dozen rabbits.

The following day he dedicated himself to preparing the meat for Aunt Catherine and Ellen to dry or smoke.

Each time he rested, the Bible was in his hand. Instead of peace, reading it stirred up the restlessness he tried hard to suppress.

He read Luke's account of the man lowered through the rooftop.

Jesus didn't hesitate. "Man, thy sins are forgiven thee."

As if that wasn't enough, Jesus read the thoughts of the Pharisees, answering their unanswered accusations with, "Is it easier to say, thy sins be forgiven thee; or to say, Rise up and walk? But that you may know that the Son of man hath power upon earth to forgive sins, He said unto the man sick of the palsy, "I say unto thee, arise, and take up thy couch, and go into thine house."

Jacob threw the Bible down. He didn't want to read anymore. The answers he wanted weren't there. Wasted time, that's what the reading was. If he knew nothing else, it was that time was too scarce to waste when he could lose someone dear at any moment. Better that he take care of their needs while he could. That was the only purpose left for his life, his only reason for being here.

He rose and limped back to his work.

CHAPTER NINE

Jacob
April 22, 1865

THE NIGHT was still. Too still. The sounds of night creatures were noticeably absent. He glanced at the men sleeping around the fire. Johnny's shock of red hair stuck straight up from beneath the blanket pulled over his head. Martin lay on his side. The men had trained him to sleep on his side to keep his snoring down.

"You will bring the enemy right to us," they used to grumble. Once, Walter went as far as sewing gum balls into the hem of Martin's night shirt to keep him off his back.

Captain Powers lay close to the rock formation. Even in sleep, his hair lay neat, his chin cleanshaven.

It was good to lie here with his fellow soldiers around him, alive and well.

A sound came from beside the wagon, and Jacob glanced toward it, reaching for his holster as he moved.

Sergeant Tanner grinned at Jacob, a stick of jerky in his hand, food retrieved from the last home they raided.

"That is part of the rations," Jacob whispered, restraining himself from snatching the jerky from the sergeant's hand. While the rest of them lived on half rations, Sergeant Tanner helped himself to supplies routinely.

The sergeant lifted a finger to his lips. "Got to have strength for the attack."

Strange light filled the clearing. Men on horseback rushed through the trees. Screaming, they waved swords above their heads.

Throwing himself on top of Johnny, Jacob felt for his gun. His hand gripped an empty holster. His knife—where were his weapons? Johnny! He grasped at his brother's blanket, pulling Johnny toward him. Dead eyes stared up at him, mouth agape. The shocking stench of decaying flesh filled his nostrils, and Jacob shoved the body away. Bony fingers grasped at his jacket, clinging, nails digging into his shirt. Jacob jerked free.

Martin sat up, his chest riddled with holes. He pointed at Jacob, lips parted and his tongue covered with flies. Martin, Walter, Captain Powers, they were all dead.

Silence returned like an evil presence. The soldiers on horseback were gone, only Sergeant Tanner remained, towering over Jacob. He bent down, grasping Jacob by the throat. Jacob gasped, kicked, and pushed, finally breaking free of Tanner's grasp. Tanner fell backward, landing with a loud thud, his face wreathed in anger, then morphing into pain.

Only it wasn't Tanner's face, it was the face of a woman.

Jacob came awake with a gasp, arms flailing and searching his bedding for something unknown.

"I am well! Be still," the woman said in a gentle Georgia drawl, concern and a bit of fear showing through the pain. "It is a night terror, is all."

Jacob blinked hard, reached a hand to wipe the sweat from his eyes. He scrambled to his feet. "Ellen! Ma'am, forgive me. Did I injure you?"

He staggered back, afraid to approach her. Shaking his head, he tried to clear it of the remnants of the nightmare. His fellow soldiers were gone. All deceased but Jacob and Sergeant Tanner. Thank God he hadn't had his gun at hand, or Ellen might be lying dead as well.

"I'm fine," the woman responded in her heavy drawl, "but you, sir, that be the third night you be crying out in your sleep. I thought maybe if I talked you through, it'd ease. I was sorely wrong."

"My apologies, ma'am." Shaken, Jacob reached to help Ellen to her feet, "I do not know what came over me. Never would I intentionally harm you. Did I awaken Ruthie?"

Ellen took his hand. "No, you did not awaken Ruthie. She could sleep through a battle. She did once. I will tell you of it sometime."

Jacob paced. The nightmares were so real and he had no control over his actions when they occurred. Was he a danger to others? He held his hands out, palms up in front of him, willing the shaking to stop.

"May I make you some tea?" He had to do something.

"Yes, I would be grateful for some tea," she said. "While my physical self is unharmed, I must admit my nerves are a bit shaken."

Jacob pulled a chair out for Ellen and then fanned the coals in the fireplace and placed some sticks on them, coaxing the blaze to rekindle. Placing the kettle of water above the flames, he returned to the shelves where his aunt kept jars of tea leaves, then waited for the kettle to boil.

"My husband, Irving Daniel William Montgomery, the third,"—Ellen lifted her brows as if saying, 'Are you impressed?'— "suffered from night terrors as well." Her fingers traced an unknown shape on the table. "Many soldiers do. I went to be with Danny, you know. At the hospital. He did not die quickly, so we were able to be together those last days."

Ellen bit her lip, studying her fingernails, then returned to tracing figures on the table.

"He never saw our baby girl. They would not allow me to bring her into the hospital to see him, so I brought the photograph of her first birthday. I had saved every penny and spent it all on that photograph, so as I could send it to my husband. Then I got his letter that he was in the hospital. I brought it in person. He was so happy, held it to his chest until he had his last breath. He passed three months after her first birthday."

Her blue eyes rose to meet his, void of tears.

The kettle boiled, and steam poured from the spout.

"The water is ready, Mr. Reddington. I could use that tea if you please."

Jacob cleared his throat, grasped a rag to protect his hand from the heat of the kettle and lifted it from the fire to rest on the hearth. While waiting, he removed the teacups from the shelf, setting one in front of Ellen and one at the end of the table for himself. Each step, carefully considered, helped his nerves regain a semblance of control.

He measured the desired portion of leaves into the pot and poured the hot water over them to steep. Studying his pocket watch, he waited. A good cup of tea would not be rushed. At last he poured, first filling Ellen's cup then his own.

"Milk?" he asked, laying a spoon beside her teacup.

She shook her head.

Ellen picked up the spoon, turning it back and forth, examining the etching in the silver handle.

"His night terrors diminished after I arrived." Ellen smiled shyly. "My husband said he could never dream ill dreams in my presence, so I insisted on staying with him. He did have dreams, Mr. Reddington, once the fever set in. Even when his mind was gone to me, his heart still called my name while he slept."

Jacob observed Ellen as she ran a finger along the rim of the teacup, round and round. She seemed a no-nonsense kind of woman: rose early, worked hard, was not given to complaining. She was also gentle and soft-spoken, especially when dealing with her daughter. Hearing her speak of her husband in the dreamy way a young girl spoke of a lover was unexpected.

"What of your woman?" she asked. "I've heard you call her at night. What is her name?"

Jacob almost lost his grip on his teacup. "What did you say?"

Ellen looked up at him, her brows drawn, confused. "Your woman. I'm sure she has a name."

"Who are you talking about?"

"It is a small house, Mr. Reddington. Not much goes on that is not heard in the next room. When finally you sleep soundly, you talk to her. I was wondering if she knew you were here."

Jacob rubbed his chin, then his forehead. Pulling out his own chair, he lowered himself with a sigh.

Ellen frowned, her color rising. "Now it is my turn to apologize, it appears I have overstepped my bounds. I had no intention of bringing up difficult memories."

Jacob shook his head, his forehead wrinkling. He stared into his cup. A few specks of tea leaves, having escaped through the filter of the pot, swirled in the amber liquid. He rubbed his chin.

Across the table, Ellen sipped her drink. She was quiet, her cheeks flushed.

Jacob cleared his throat.

"No need for apologies, ma'am. It is just, well, the woman in my dreams—I do not know her name."

There. He said it. Let Ellen take him for the fool he was, falling for some woman he had never met.

Ellen's eyes flew wide, and she clapped her hands with delight. "I must hear all about her! This mysterious woman without a name has clearly left an impact on you. Please tell. Perhaps I can help you find her."

"You would think me daft."

"No. I believe in love at first sight. My Danny and I, we knew we were meant for each other when first we met."

"That is the problem," Jacob lifted the teacup, wishing it were large enough to hide behind. "This woman–you say I speak to her at night? Out loud?"

Ellen nodded with the enthusiasm of a young child.

Jacob stared into his cup. "We have never met. I have never seen her—except when I dream."

Ellen tilted her head to one side, studying him through hooded eyes. "So, this woman, whom you have never met, is in your dreams often? Always the same person?"

"Yes, yes. I swear I must be insane. I know she is a figment of my imagination, but she seems so real. Sometimes when I sing with her, her eyes turn toward me as though she senses I am there, and it eases her."

"It eases her? Is she in distress? In your dreams?"

"She is looking for someone, someone lost to her, I believe, although I do not know if I heard her say that or I am simply drawing a conclusion. I know, I know. It cannot be real. But somehow I know she *is* real, and when I see her, I feel like my life has a purpose. I long to find her, but do not know how."

Ellen shook her head. "Dear boy, your life has a purpose, whether it includes finding this woman or otherwise. God would not have sustained you had He not had a reason for doing so. I suggest you search for what purpose that is. Perhaps then these night terrors will cease."

Jacob took a long, steady drink of his tea, ignoring the burning on the roof of his mouth. "I have failed at all I have purposed to do until now. What use am I to God?"

Ellen reached a hand and covered his. Her fingers were rough with callouses, her nails broken and uneven. "Oh, Jacob," she said as a mother speaks to admonish a child, "perhaps you are trying too hard to do things on your own. If I be reading my Bible correctly, it says to not lean on our own understanding. In all our ways we are to acknowledge Him, and then He will direct where we should go. He knows where you are, and He knows where He wants you to go. Follow His lead."

Jacob stood so abruptly he almost knocked over the chair. "So, that is what you did? Acknowledged God, and He led you to, what? Here? A widow? Alone?"

"I am not alone, Jacob! Yes, I am a widow, but I have loved and been loved more deeply than most who lived a lifetime. I have Ruthie and your Aunt Catherine—who is more family to me than I ever dreamed a family could be. I work hard with my hands, and it is a joy I never knew until necessity brought me to it. My life is in God's hands, and I see His hand in everything that happens around me. I would not change my life for a million alternatives. And you know what else? I can sleep at night, and I know no matter what evil is out there, I can trust God to do what is best for me and my little girl."

Silence echoed throughout the room, Ellen's words reverberating in Jacob's mind as he stared out the window. Just last evening he had read that same verse in Mrs. Powers's Bible. *In all thy ways acknowledge him and he will direct your paths.* What did that mean? Knowing God existed didn't seem to encompass the full meaning. How do you acknowledge God in all your ways?

The moon shone full, outlining the tall trees against a shadowy mist. From the shed behind the house he could hear the soft clucking of hens, other mothers soothing their children in the dark. Grasping his hat, Jacob punched the inside with his fist.

"I thank you, ma'am." He bowed in Ellen's direction. "You give me much to consider."

He reached for the doctor's Bible that lay beside his bedroll, then bolted out the front door and headed into the fog of the night. It was time he and God had a conversation.

CHAPTER TEN

Wrestling with God

ANGUISH TORE at Jacob's soul as he knelt on the bank of the river.

It was a cruel joke. Suffering upon suffering, only to be left behind. Hadn't he paid enough? God could have saved Johnny if He'd wanted to. Was God even there? No. If He had been there—Johnny would not have died. Not just Johnny, but the others. So many good men died. Jacob shook his fist. "Did You kill him because of me? Why? Take me instead!"

Hours passed, and the energy Jacob had spent blaming himself erupted into an anger toward God that Jacob never before allowed himself to express. No longer able to hold it all in, he poured out his rage, not caring if God struck him dead for blasphemy. He ranted and pounded his fists against his chest, beat the ground, demanded a response. Waited for lightning to strike.

But God did not answer.

"Why?" He cried out, "Why did You let me live?"
Silence.

He never once questioned God's existence, never doubted the might and omniscience of his creator. It was the Almighty's character that Jacob doubted.

"You say You are a God of love. Really? How far would You go to prove it, because I don't believe You. If You are as powerful and good as You say You are, none of this would have happened."

His father had been a man of incredible faith, living every day of his life imitating what he called "a God who loves beyond understanding," a God who gave His son to save the world, a God who had a plan for the lives of His children, for good and not for harm. He saw the same childlike trust flow in his aunt's life. He wanted that, and hated himself for the wanting.

Did God pick and choose whom He loved? Was that kind of faith unique to only those chosen few?

A verse from Jacob's last reading came in that clear, almost audible voice. *Simon, Simon, behold, Satan hath desired to have you, that he may sift you as wheat.* A shiver ran up his spine. *But I have prayed for thee, that thy faith fail not, and when thou art converted, strengthen thy brethren.*

Jacob knelt, silent, his body trembling.

"God of my father?" he whispered into the night.

The wind moved through the trees. All was silent except for the call of night creatures.

He thought of the Roman centurion who believed Jesus could heal his servant without being present. He thought of the Jewish father who stood before Jesus with the demon-tortured child, willing to ask for help but not believing Jesus would answer his plea.

"Lord, I do not understand. I kneel here pleading, yet not believing You will answer." Tremendous fatigue washed over Jacob. He collapsed on the ground. The smell of the earth filled his nostrils. Dampness cooled his tear-streaked cheeks. The ache in his wounded leg throbbed from the hours on his knees. He was tired of fighting. He longed to surrender. Instead, he turned his face upward, clenched his fist, and shook it at the starry sky winking through the branches overhead.

"I want to trust You as my father did, but I cannot." Why should he?

The rustling of leaves was the only response.

What had God ever done for him? Trust came easily once, as naive youth often experienced. He had trusted his father's God, until that father was gone and there was no one to whose faith he could hold on.

I am the God of your Father. I will be your God.

He wanted this so badly he felt his insides would tear. For so many years, he had gone through the motions, not knowing how to make it personal. For so long, not caring.

Despair washed over him. He needed to end his resistance. Let God do what He wished, for better or worse, Jacob would fight no more. He lowered his face to the ground, no strength left to even hold up his head.

"I believe. Help my unbelief. I surrender. Do as You please, be it to let me live or to let me die."

Take my yoke upon you, and learn of me; for I am meek and lowly of heart: and ye shall find rest unto your soul.

Jacob's Path

Like a warm wind whispering over him, heat crept over Jacob's prostrate form. He lay motionless. This was new. Different. His hands and feet tingled, and peace engulfed him. What was this?

Raising his face, Jacob let the gentle breeze caress his cheeks. Awe filled his mind, and his heart expanded in his chest.

Behold, I am with you always. Even unto the end of the world.

Jacob knew the voice, and his soul responded.

"Thank You, Father. You are my God. I am Yours. Show me Your path, and I will follow."

This time the tears contained a newfound joy he could not describe.

The night was no longer dark, the night critters' song no longer hopeless. Jacob lay still and listened until their song diminished, giving way to the sounds of morning.

There on the side of the river, as the first rays of sun peeked over the hills, he fell into a deep and undisturbed sleep.

The sun was well past the meridian when Jacob awoke. The sky above him shone clear, the air was alive. Small animals scampered through the brush, birds sang, and the smell of dirt and water permeated the air.

Jacob took a deep breath and stretched. It felt good. It felt like life. He flexed his arms, feeling the muscles tighten, and then extended them out again. His legs straightened, toes extended. He felt good. Too good.

He stretched his leg again, turned his foot to the right, to the left, toes up, toes down. Every fiber was invigorated.

With slow movements, Jacob drew himself to sitting. There were no sharp jabs. Nothing ached. He rubbed his wounded calf, raised the pant leg and rubbed again. The scars were faded, dull as wounds from long ago, undeniable evidence of the shrapnel once there. Below the scars, muscle bulged, healthy and unharmed.

CHAPTER ELEVEN

Peace
April 26, 1865

THE WOODPILE loomed high and thick in neat stacks against the barn. Jacob hadn't needed to stop to rest his leg once since that night alone with God. His shoulders and axe arm, however, cramped in protest after hours of effort. He rubbed his shoulder and grinned. There was enough wood to last the ladies through the next winter. The garden was now plowed to almost double its former size and planting had begun. Meat hung in the smokehouse.

Much had been accomplished, and he felt good.

It was time to leave. He wasn't sure where he was going. He'd been praying about it pretty much without ceasing.

I will lead you home in time, the voice had said.

Jacob cringed. His mother would not welcome him back, but if that was the path God was leading him to, he would go.

He glanced up at the angle of the sun, grasped his pack, and settled down in the shade of a tree.

He was hungry, not for food, but to read.

Learn of me and ye shall find rest.

Every spare moment he spent reading Sofia's Bible and journal. He flipped through the Bible pages until he came to the chapter that made his heart soar.

Psalm 103

"Bless the Lord, O my soul: and all that is within me, bless his holy name. Bless the Lord, O my soul, and forget not all his benefits: who forgiveth all thine iniquities: who healeth all thy diseases; who redeemeth thy life from destruction; who crowneth thee with lovingkindness and tender mercies;"

The whole chapter was permanently embedded in his mind. Still, seeing the words written in front of him brought an extra spark of excitement. He skimmed down to verse ten and continued, feeling a thrill in his heart like none he had ever known.

"He hath not dealt with us after our sins; nor rewarded us according to our iniquities. For as the heaven is high above the earth, so great is his mercy toward them that fear him. As far as the east is from the west, so far hath he removed our transgressions from us."

Lifting his face toward the sky, Jacob closed his eyes. His heart still ached every time he thought of Johnny, but overriding the pain was a comfort and peace. God was in control.

"If you wish to sleep, I am sure the house would be more comfortable." Ellen's voice interrupted his thoughts.

Jacob opened one eye, squinting up at her.

"Brought you some berry pie. Last can of the preserves we squirreled away last year. Fresh berries should be ripe in another month or so." She handed him a plate and lowered herself to the ground, leaning against the tree. Her sleeve fluttered against his arm as she leaned forward, smoothing out her skirt.

"Much obliged," Jacob grinned, taking a fork full.

"You are a new man, Jacob Reddington." She nodded at the Bible open on his lap. "What happened to you, that night you fled from the house?"

"I wrestled with God. He won."

"Like Jacob in the Bible."

"Yes." Jacob rubbed his leg, still amazed at how different he felt. He understood entirely the phrase, "being born again."

"But unlike my namesake, I rose with my leg healed instead of lame, an outer demonstration of what He has done to me on the inside."

There was a long silence as Ellen observed Jacob.

"Have you found your purpose in life, Mr. Reddington?" she asked.

"Aside from chopping wood and seeing as you women have food to last a while? Not yet."

"Hmmm."

"But it is in God's hands. I am waiting for His directions." Jacob took another bite of pie.

"No night terrors of late, I noticed." She continued to study him.

"No. I have slept well."

"Still dreaming of the nameless woman." It was a statement, not a question.

Jacob focused on his plate, breaking off a piece of pie with his fork. It was a mystery why God took away the nightmares, but still allowed those dreams to fill his nights. He glanced at Ellen, unsure of what to say. He knew his aunt hoped he would become interested in Ellen, and Ellen had been very attentive. Yet he felt no emotion but thankfulness for her kindness. "I do."

"Tell me of her."

Fork halfway to his mouth, Jacob paused. "Why?"

"Come now, it will not hurt my feelings. I know your aunt hoped to get us courting, but—" She paused, looking off across the field, her work-roughened hand brushing a strand of hair from her eyes, "I know what it is to fall in love, and whereas you are as fine a man as any, I do not feel toward you what I did when I met my husband. Besides, I cannot, nor have I the desire to compete with a dream woman. Still, I am curious."

His face heated, and she laughed.

"Humor me," she said. I feel like hearing something sweet. You were humming in your sleep last night. Were you singing to her?"

"You mock me."

"No. Honest. Tell me what you dreamt."

"It is difficult to describe. She is an odd woman, not like any I have known. She dresses in a most peculiar fashion—with trousers like a man, but she is quite feminine."

"I have heard of women out west who wear men's pants. I often thought it would be easier to tend to my chores if I did not have all these layers of skirt to deal with. Does she dress like that?"

"Yes, but her clothes are different from ours. Simpler. She must be from another part of the world. She wears her hair plain, either loose or tied at the back of her neck like a child. She is beautiful, with eyes as black as the night. I sometimes wish the dream would go on and on so I could watch her."

"It is not polite to spy on an innocent young woman, Mr. Reddington." Her eyes showed she was teasing. She clapped her hands together. "Now go on. What did you dream last night that made you sing?"

Jacob sighed. Each dream was vivid, as if he were there, and the memories remained fresh and strong. "She frequents a place by a river. It makes her sad each time, like it is full of memories she wishes to hold on to. She sits on the edge of the stream, with her feet in the cool of the water, and she hums a melody. I hum it with her. It makes her smile when I do."

"Can you sing it to me?"

"There are no words, just a melody."

"I am listening."

Jacob closed his eyes, seeking the tune he already knew well, letting the music carry him. When he opened his eyes, a tear rolled down Ellen's cheek.

"That is beautiful. I have never heard that melody, or any like it."

"Neither have I, except in my dreams," Jacob said. "However, it must be a known piece. The lady doctor, the one who gave me this—" Jacob lifted the Bible from his lap, turned it from side to side, and laid it back down. "She recognized the melody and wanted to talk with me about how I came about knowing the music, but she never said how she learned it."

"That is curious."

They relaxed, each lost in thought.

Jacob interrupted their reverie. "Did Aunt Catherine make it back from the general store? I didn't hear her return."

"You were chopping wood. She and Ruthie are in the kitchen. She sent me out with the pie and told me to have you go in when you were done sleeping like the bum you are."

Ellen slapped his arm and giggled like a schoolgirl. Getting to her feet, she shaded her eyes and gazed at the house.

"The song, it makes one feel a longing, does it not? Now you have messed with my mood, Mr. Reddington. I best return to the house lest your aunt start calling me a loafer as well. Are you done with that?" She pointed at his plate.

Jacob scraped the last of the pie from the plate, picked up his Bible and the plate, and rose. "I will take it in myself and see what she wants."

They both laughed and sauntered toward the house, the afternoon breeze refreshing against his sweat-dampened shirt.

"That you, Jakie?" Aunt Catherine's voice called out as soon as his boot touched the threshold.

"It is." Jacob peered into the room.

Aunt Catherine was elbow-deep in bread dough, Ruthie at her side. Flour covered the little girl's face, and she grinned up at him.

He winked, taking his boots off at the door then depositing his plate and fork onto the table. Sauntering to his aunt, he placed a kiss on her flushed cheek and flicked a speck of dough off Ruthie's forehead.

"Good. I could use some help with your uncle's fowling gun." She nodded at the shotgun nestled on its ledge above the doorframe. "If you can clean it well and oil it for me, I would be much appreciative. I have neglected the old piece since afore you arrived. By the way, a man has been asking about you in town. Said he was a friend of yours."

"Who would that be?"

"Sheriff Riley said he did not seem an honest fellow, so he told him you left for home a few days back. Seems to me our sheriff is not being honest himself, but I trust him. Does the name Tanner mean anything to you? Jethro Tanner?"

Jacob's stomach tightened. "I know him. He was in my unit in the army."

"Hmm. Well now." Aunt Catherine turned back to kneading dough.

Jacob stood, expecting her to say more. She leaned into her work, turning and punching the dough. After a moment she glanced up at him. "The gun?"

"You plan on shooting bird?"

"Might chase off some vultures if they come this way."

He laughed, but uneasiness curled around his gut. Why would Jethro be looking for him? Jacob hoped to keep reminders of those dark days way behind him. Still, they had fought side by side, and on more than one occasion survived the battle with the other's help. Was Jethro the vulture Aunt Catherine planned to keep away? Naw, the old house was clearly free of any wealth that would draw Jethro's attention.

Cleaning a space on the side table, Jacob spread out a cloth and retrieved the cleaning materials to tend to the shotgun.

Ellen's soft drawl caught his attention. She was a pretty thing. He had hardly noticed the fine lines of her neck, her slender waist.

Jethro would notice.

He reached over his head to bring down the gun from its place. His uncle had insisted that a gun belonged where grown folks could access it with ease should the need arise. Aunt Catherine kept up the over-the-door tradition.

As if reading his mind, his aunt interrupted. "Feels good to have the gun back in its place. They were confiscating weapons during the war, you know. I could not imagine my husband would have surrendered his, so neither did I."

"How did they not take it?"

"I hid it in the cellar, in a wooden box like those used to bury children. In case that were not enough,

I kept the sack of rotting vegetables atop it." She shook her head, chuckling. "It got to smelling so bad I could hardly go down the cellar myself—and not a single soldier or bushwacker lingered long enough to find any of the things I hid below."

Jacob shook his head. His admiration for his aunt's courage and ingenuity grew every day.

"Were you not fearful? Both to be without protection and of what would happen if it was found? They burned people's homes for less."

"There were times I would wake in the middle of the night and feel I could not breathe, I was so overwhelmed with the dangers that surrounded us. This was especially true after Ellen and Ruthie joined me. I feared harm would come to them because of choices I made. But I was not without protection. God is husband to the widow, father to the fatherless. I sought solace and wisdom in the pages that now console you."

Aunt Catherine straightened, wiping floured hands across her apron. A tear glistened in the corner of her eye. "I am a practical woman, Jacob my boy, and now, as I can have my gun, I plan to have it at the ready. Two women living alone need what protection they can get, and it is time for you to be on your way."

CHAPTER TWELVE

April 27, 1865
Where He Leads

J*ACOB READJUSTED* the strap to his pack so it didn't rub. The satchel he wore hanging at his side, where he could easily access its contents. Pausing, he glanced over his shoulder.

They stood huddled together on the front porch, Aunt Catherine, Ellen, and Ruthie. He knew his aunt would remain there, one hand over her heart, the other blocking the sun from her eyes, watching until he passed the curve of the road and was no longer visible. She seemed so frail, vulnerable. He hated to leave her but knew he must.

"God brought you here," Aunt Catherine said when she hugged him good-bye. "He knew we needed each other. Now His purpose for you here is accomplished, so feel no qualms leaving. He is watching over us."

She sighed, grasped his hands in her gnarled ones. "I never told you what your father told me after you were born, did I?"

"What was that?"

"Red said God gave you your name."

Jacob felt a jolt deep inside, hearing the nickname his dad carried. Whereas Jacob acquired the same nickname by a shortening of his surname, his father's came from his one feature everyone noticed—his hair.

Even after more than a decade, thinking of his father caused his heart to ache.

"God spoke to my father?"

"It was not a voice loud from Heaven, no trumpet call or even thunder—but a stillness your father recognized and understood. Your name came with a promise. Red both treasured and pondered its meaning."

Jacob swallowed past the lump in his throat. He could still picture his father, bent over his work, flaming red hair untamed except when hidden under his hat. He could hear him speaking out loud when he thought no one was near, conversing with God as one would to an earthly companion.

"What—what promise?"

"Like Jacob of old," Aunt Catherine quoted, "I will lead him into a strange and distant land. I will be his God, and he will be my child."

Tears swelled in her blue eyes. Aunt Catherine clasped Jacob's face in her palms and kissed his cheek. "Go, and may God bring you home once more."

Nearing the curve in the road, Jacob turned and waved to the cluster of women, before moving forward, humming to himself.

"I am ready to move on," he said out loud, imitating his memory of his father.

He walked until he got hungry, then stopped to eat some of the bread he'd packed. He read while he ate. Sofia's journal was fascinating. The lady had quite the imagination, and her work rivaled any fiction book available. Jacob shook his head at her descriptions of buildings so tall you had to crane your neck to see the sky above them. He laughed at how she recounted her run-in with the family of Indians who found her by the springs. He could see how she would be haughty enough to not want to perform the everyday tasks. It was obvious she was a lady accustomed to fine things. Yet—

Jacob remembered how tenderly she cared for those lying sick and injured, not shrinking from the ugly tasks required. Her carriage and manner marked her as one from high society, yet she was humble enough to get her hands dirty in the midst of the worst filth. Humble enough to care about the end of a man who deserved no kindness.

Fascinated, Jacob read on, page after page, losing track of time. The sun climbed higher in the sky. If he left out the time travel part, her story was vivid and rang with truth.

She wrote about running away from her husband. *"I could not be part of his plan. While taking advantage of the hospitality extended us, he wanted nothing more than to map out the locations and valuables of homes in the vicinity of future battles. I know Roger. He seeks power and he seeks wealth. He will use the war and use this knowledge to take everything he can from people who can't defend themselves. While the men are at war, how many women and children will be at home, defenseless? I shudder to think of them in Roger's hands. Heaven help them if they resist."*

Jacob closed his eyes, exhaling a shuddering breath. Captain Powers had an uncanny ability of striking the homes that possessed unusual belongings, and yes, Jacob witnessed many innocent women and children suffer to feed the captain's greed.

"Forgive me again, please, God," Jacob whispered, the old sense of shame overwhelming him. "We did so many things…"

As far as the East is from the West, so far hath he removed our transgressions.

Jacob smiled as the verse from his morning reading came back to him, bringing with it a renewed sense of peace. Was this what it meant to hear God's voice?

A twig snapped behind him, and Jacob rolled to his side, pistol drawn.

"Hello, Red."

Lowering his gun, Jacob rose to greet the man coming from the shadows of the wood.

"Hello, Sergeant."

CHAPTER THIRTEEN

April 27
Jethro

"J*ETHRO*. J*UST* J*ETHRO*. The war is over, no more Sergeant for me." Jethro Tanner smiled, showing teeth blackened by tobacco and rot. "You are a hard man to find."

Jacob reached for the leather satchel and slid Sofia's journal back inside. "I was just leaving."

"Where are you going?" Jethro eyed the satchel.

Jacob's brows rose as he took a deep breath then released it slowly. "I do not know." It was the truth.

"Mind if I join you?"

Jacob shrugged his shoulders. He didn't particularly care for Jethro's company but had no reason to turn him away.

"Ain't it most troublesome figuring what to do next? It be like fighting is all I is good for anymore." Jethro fell into step beside Jacob.

"You are healthy. Surely you can find work that suits you. And your army pension should get you through until you get on your feet if you are careful."

"Is that what you are doing? Relying on your pension?" Jethro eyed Jacob's satchel.

"My family has a farm. I expect there will be work aplenty."

"I met some of your family."

Jacob stiffened.

"In truth, I did not *meet* meet them, more as had an encounter. I learnt you had a relation living in these parts and figured you would be there, so I decided to visit and see how you are recovering. I see you have recovered well. Not even a limp."

"Encounter?" Halting his steps, Jacob narrowed his eyes at Jethro.

"Your folk ain't very hospitable. Before I got foot on the steps this shotgun goes pointing out the window and straight at me and this ugly old lady pops her head out and tells me to be on my way."

Jacob turned his head to hide his smile. "My aunt is not ugly."

"Well, she is no beauty, and I knows when I am not welcome. Asides, I figured if you was there you'da come out to greet me, us being old friends and all. So I left without another word. Was easy enough tracking you from there."

"What do you want, Jethro?"

"Ah, nothing. Just, well, I dislike being alone and I thought, you being the only other man from our unit as made it out, well..." Jethro stared at his feet, eyes dejected, shoulders slumped. "I have nowhere to go."

Jacob studied the man in front of him, feeling sympathy for him. He knew what it felt like to be lost and alone. He reached over and clasped Jethro's shoulder. "I am wandering myself. You are welcome to join me."

He regretted it within the quarter of an hour.

"You remember the Battle at Kirksville? Our men met up with McNeil's troops, and them confederated were hiding like the rodents they were—out in the cornfields, in folks' cellars, and all, you recall?"

Jacob remembered.

"They was hiding out there like cowards and the cap'n, he sure was smart, our cap'n. He suggested McNeil get some volunteers to march around to see if he could get them spineless men to start shootin' so as we could find them."

Jacob remembered. He remembered it all.

"They goes running off over the fence, and they start shooting at us from the courthouse. They outnumbered us by more than two to one. But we beat 'em. We beat 'em good."

Jacob remembered. He remembered the cannon fire, the smell of gunpowder, the ringing in his ear when the rifle fired. He could still see the bodies, broken and bleeding, draped over the fence rails, in the fields, on the porch steps of houses.

He paused, wiping sweat from his brow he glowered at his companion. "I wish not to speak of the war. If you insist on reminiscing, leave me out of it."

Still Jethro babbled on. Jacob increased his pace.

"You recall the house we cleared not far from there? Harboring traitors, they were. They had quite a stash of jewelry. The cap'n was supposed to split it with us, said he would at the end. He say anything to you about that?"

Jacob shook his head.

"I find it mighty strange, you being the only one to survive, and you being the only one to talk with the cap'n at the end."

"It was not my choice to be there."

"You sure he told you nothing? I figure he did, but you just waited till he be dead, and now you are the only one as knows where he hid the treasure. I figure if I ever want my share, I need to accompany you until it is found."

Sliding the pack off his shoulder, Jacob felt the rush of hot blood flood his cheeks. His fists tightened, ready to swing. "I take that as an insult to my character."

"Whoa!" Jethro raised his hands in front of him, palms forward. "I was jesting. My apologies, didna mean to get you all riled up. You know me, Red, sometimes I say all the wrong things. Yore right, of course. I never knew you to be other than upright and honest."

"See that you do not say such things again."

"I promise. I will watch my tongue."

He must have meant it, because Jethro remained quiet for the next couple of hours as they walked.

"This is my neck of the woods," Jethro said, nodding to the east of them. "Our family used to own a farm that way, afore we moved to the city."

"Do you wish to return and see if it is standing?"

"No. Nothing there I want to see."

Leaving the road, Jacob followed a path that descended between some rocky bluffs. The trees grew thick and tall, and the shadow of the bluffs blocked the warmth of the sun.

Jethro shivered.

"Down there is Witch's Creek. You sure you want to be heading that way?"

"That is the way I am going."

Jethro shook his head. "Place is haunted. Some Injuns live nearby, say they are the guardians of the spring. It is a sacred place to them—some entry into the spirit world."

"I do not believe in ghosts."

"I heard some stories—"

"You can leave if you wish. To me, the thought of setting camp near a freshwater spring sounds perfect."

Drawing his jacket close, Jethro didn't reply but followed closely behind. The terrain was rough and rocky. The difficult descent, made easier by steps carved into the side of the rock wall, required full concentration. If it weren't for the steps, Jacob would think the valley floor untouched by humans. The hunting down here was probably excellent.

Once on the level ground, he followed a deer path, weaving back and forth around massive trees. Roots jutted through the dirt, waiting to trip any who didn't watch their step. The path opened to a clearing, and Jacob paused to take in the view. Bluffs stood both behind him and in front, with a fast-moving creek gurgling in between.

"We will camp here tonight," Jacob said, smiling. Already his feet tingled with anticipation of wading into the shallow water.

Jethro frowned. "Witch's Creek." He shook his head, mumbling to himself. "He brought us right to Witch's Creek."

Dropping their packs to the ground, the two began to make camp. The canvas used for shelter was set up with the ease of men for whom this had become a habit.

"I will find dry wood." Jethro nodded in the direction of the trees. "You prepare the pit for the fire."

Jacob set to digging a hole and collecting rock with which to line it. The rock had to be selected with care. Some river rocks could pop and shatter under the intense heat, creating shrapnel as dangerous as shotgun fire.

On completing the pit, Jacob glanced about, admiring his surroundings. Maybe he could get washed up before Jethro returned.

A tree lay close to the creek bed, leaning lazily as if attempting to drink from the cool water with its branches. He stripped off his boots, coat, and shirt, and swung them over the branches where they could stay dry and be within easy reach. With his pant legs rolled to his knees, he stepped into the water.

The coolness felt good to his aching feet. The water swirled around his ankles as he stepped, taking care not to slip on the rocks. Bending over, he scooped handfuls of the clear liquid and doused his face and head. Wiping his eyes, he caught movement from shore.

Jethro was back, and in his hands was Jacob's leather satchel.

"Drop it, Jethro," Jacob said, pushing the hair back from his face.

"Not happening. Seems if you guard something so carefully, there must be something of value in it. You reckon the captain left directions to where he hid his treasure in this here book?" Opening the satchel, Jethro reached in and pulled out Sofia's journal.

"That is not the captain's." Jacob wiped water from his face, blinking away drops of water from his eyes. He waded to the overhanging branches where his clothes hung. How could he be so careless? *Keep these away from him, please,* Sofia had said. *In the wrong hands, they could make trouble for me.*

He could not let Jethro read the journal.

"One of those is a Bible. A Bible, you hear? That's not exactly where the captain would keep a list of his crimes. Not even he would do that."

"I think you be hiding something from me. What will it be? We gonna share them treasures, right? We done the work together. It's only right we share them. That is, if you play nice."

We done the work together. Jacob shuddered. *Lord, how many times do I need to ask forgiveness before I believe You? What would You have me do?*

"May I get dressed first?" Jacob's mind raced as he reached for his shirt. One sleeve dipped into the water.

We will be more clever than he. From the looks of him, that won't be hard. Sofia's words rang in his ears.

He had to think, buy some time. Hating to take his eyes off Jethro, he hurried to pull the shirt over his head, tugging the dripping sleeve into place. He slipped his wet feet into his boots, and with a sigh picked up the coat, snapping it in the air to remove any leaves.

"You can have the Captain's treasures, Jethro. I told you, those aren't his books. They belonged to his wife."

Jethro's eyebrows shot high.

"His wife? What wife? Why'd she give them to you? You reckon as she knew where he hid his stuff?"

"No. I do not reckon she did. Jethro, if you put down those books, I might be able to help you. Let me have my bag and my books. There be nothing there for you."

Jethro leered, his teeth a blackened smudge across his face. Lifting Sofia's journal, he stepped toward the creek bed. "How much this one worth to you? Reckon a swim in the creek be something you want it to avoid?" His brows drew together, and his leer turned into a scowl.

"Maybe this will persuade you." Slipping his other hand into the satchel, he pulled out Jacob's revolver.

Jacob groaned. How could he be so foolish?

One hand holding Jacob's pistol, Jethro's other held the journal between thumb and forefinger. "Start talking."

Slipping on a rock, Jacob grasped the branch beside him, his eyes shooting toward the water. His heart froze. A reflection not his own shimmered below him. *Her* reflection. He blinked. The girl from his dreams.

"I said, start talking."

He couldn't let Jethro read the journal. Jacob glanced back at the reflection, his heart lurching. He stared, his mouth dry.

"I am not a patient man, Jacob."

He tore his eyes from the vision in the water. Jethro clasped the book, hand pulled back as though ready to toss it into the creek.

"No!" Jacob had promised. He had to protect the journal.

Lunging for Jethro's outstretched hand, he grasped the journal.

The overpowering and familiar stench of sulfur and burning charcoal filled the air. At the same time as the boom of the gun, a punch to his shoulder propelled him backward toward the water. Jacob fell, pulling the journal with him.

And he kept falling.

Jethro's eyes widened with confusion and terror as his body twisted, one hand still clinging to the journal, he fell along with him. Together, they plummeted into a blackness unlike any Jacob had ever known.

The darkness tore at him, cold and burning, twisting, compressing. He felt like his insides were exploding as he spun, falling, falling. He reached for Jethro, for the sides of whatever this was. Jacob tried to grasp for anything of substance, but his hands gripped emptiness. He screamed, hearing nothing except the pressing vastness of silence, his voice swallowed into the terrifying spin of darkness.

Was this death?

CHAPTER FOURTEEN

She Wrote the Truth

COMING TO, Jacob gasped, his nostrils full of the scent of damp and rotting leaves. Dirt caked his lips, and grit pressed against his tongue. He blinked, aware of the cool tug of water against his legs.

"Oh." A moan escaped his lips.

He was freezing. Sunlight edged through the green leaves of a large oak tree, sprinkling the ground with odd shapes and shadows. It had the look of summer, but he was cold deep into his very bones. It was as cold as the last winter when supplies were low, their boots worn and full of holes. The only way to stay warm was to share his blanket with Johnny and huddle beneath.

But he had no blanket, and Johnny was gone.

He shivered. Where was he?

Jethro. He recalled the look on Jethro's face as they plummeted into—into what? The abyss? He groaned once again, turning on his side to see where he lay.

If this was hell, it looked an awful lot like Missouri. A cold Missouri.

The shivering worsened. Jacob spat dirt from his mouth, pushing himself to his knees. A sharp pain shot through his upper arm.

"Blast him." Glancing at his arm, he took in the ooze of blood, the stained sleeve. He recalled the smell of gunpowder, the echo of his gun, the punch to his arm. A surge of anger welled in his chest.

"You shot me. Jethro, you shot me! When I get my hands on you—"

He'd tried to save Sofia's journal. He glanced about. A dull ache pressed into his–knee? Wait, no, something *was* pressing into his knee. A book. The journal. He was atop the journal. *Thank you, Lord.*

Kicking booted feet, Jacob crawled to dryer ground. There, in a patch of sunlight, he drew his legs close, trying to control the violent shivers that wracked his body.

"Control yourself, Reddington," he muttered through clenched teeth. "Check the book, check the book, man."

Dreading what he would find, Jacob sat upright and forced his shaking fingers to open the journal. He took a deep breath, amazed. Dry. It was dry.

I must be hallucinating.

Trees spun in great dizzying circles. Lowering his head between his knees, he forced himself to breathe deep, filling his lungs with air.

A narrow inlet of water formed a calm pool lined by a bank of sand and rocks. Scraped into the surface he could see where he had dragged himself from the water and collapsed on the shore. Beyond the sandbar moved a fast-coursing river. The landmarks were familiar, like something left from a dream, or a long ago memory. The rocks rising on the other side of the river were similar to those beside the creek bed he had been at moments before. Witch's Creek, Jethro called it.

How? How came I to this place? So cold. I am so cold. I need to stanch the bleeding. Then get warm.

He clutched the journal to his chest, thought better of it, and wiping his hand across to remove any dirt, placed it away from him. With trembling fingers, he reached to inspect the burning in his forearm, pulling the shirt away from the wound, allowing his breath to whistle between clenched teeth.

He couldn't believe Jethro had shot him. After years of fighting side by side, how could the man do this to him?

A deep groove sliced through just below the bulge of muscles of his upper arm. White flesh glistened below drying blood. Rivulets of red-tinged water dripped down the length of his arm. Prodding around the wound, Jacob grunted. "Just a flesh wound. No bone, no bullet. You seen worse, old boy. A bandage will prevent more bleeding. Now, where is your bag?"

His gaze traveled along the shoreline, then out toward the river. He felt a sudden urge to see if *her* face would be reflected in the quiet water here as it had been in the shallow creek bed.

"You are indeed hallucinating, Jacob Reddington," he scolded himself.

That was when he saw Jethro. Bobbing back and forth, face up, his body was caught against a fallen tree near the rush of water. His boots, tugged by the current, pulled him down until his torso dipped under the surface. Then the branches, ever resisting the pull, would push him back to the surface. Soon, the current would dislodge him from the tree and pull him in the rest of the way.

"He deserves it." Jacob rose to his feet as he spoke. He caught his breath and forced his eyes to focus against the spinning forest. With unsteady feet he stepped into the clear, cold water. The branch holding Jethro bent ever so slightly. It could break anytime, releasing both branch and Jethro into the current.

"Let him die. He deserves no less," Jacob grumbled to himself. Still he moved forward, feeling oddly steadied by the water tugging about him.

"Who knows how far downstream we were carried. He is probably dead already."

The shallow pool dropped away suddenly, and Jacob found himself wading through chest-deep water. He could feel the pull of the current. Memories of his father flashed through his mind. Knowing the danger, his father never hesitated.

Jacob moved closer to the fallen tree, grasping the arm of his fellow soldier.

Jethro was alive. The fall and rise of his chest left little ripples in the water beside him. Blood caked the top of his head.

Jacob reached for him, untangling the wild strands of hair from a branch. He pulled, but Jethro didn't move.

Across his shoulders lay a leather strap, now caught on some unseen limbs below him. Jacob grasped his shirt and pulled. He felt more than he heard the pop as the branch broke and Jethro began to sink, dragged under by the weight of the bag. Jacob's bag.

Somehow he dragged Jethro back to the shore. Bandaging Jethro's wound, feeling his pulse beating strong and his breathing easy, Jacob knew Jethro would survive.

Leaving the yet unconscious man safely on shore, Jacob followed a road away from the river. Out of the woods he wandered, until he reached a clearing; a square of sorts, with nothing but scattered trees lining its perimeter and a strange, dome-shaped contraption beside a set of tables bound together by smooth bands of steel. The grass was lush, and the sun shone on a series of benches made of concrete, inviting him to rest and be warmed.

He sat, and the heat of the sun-drenched bench soaked into his chilled and aching bones. Opening his bag and removing each of his belongings, Jacob spread them out, allowing the sunshine to dry them. Removing the oiled skin from Sofia's Bible, he rifled through the pages. Only a few damp pages. He sighed, holding it in his hands, feeling the warmth that filled him every time he held it. He opened the pages and bowed his head.

"Lord, I have no idea what has happened to me," he said out loud. He marveled at how easy praying came for him these last few days. "I would appreciate it if You helped me out with this one."

She wrote the truth. The thought echoed in his head as he stared down at the doctor's journal. She'd written about falling through the river, much the same way he had.

Through time?

A squirrel scurried from a branch overhead and leaped across to another. No one was in sight. Raising a brow, Jacob ran his hand across his forehead, rubbed his chin, and squinted at the sky.

Sofia wrote the truth. He couldn't shake the thought.

A chill ran up Jacob's spine.

"Lord, am I daft in the head? Because if what she said is true, I am in deep trouble."

Another verse from scripture came to mind. *Behold, I send an angel before you on the way and to bring you to the place I have prepared.*

CHAPTER FIFTEEN

June 2, 2014
Officer Walker

JACOB AWAKENED with a start as rough hands grabbed his shoulders, shaking him. Above him loomed a man in uniform. *A confederate!*

Grasping the man's arms, Jacob wrestled him to the ground, rolled on top of him, pinning his arms behind his back and holding him firmly against the ground with a knee to the back.

"Who are you and what is your purpose here?" Jacob demanded. "Are you with the Union or rebels?"

"I am with the sheriff's department, and you are assaulting an officer of the law." The man below him was angry. Very angry.

Still gripping the man's wrists behind his back, Jacob looked him over. The uniform was not that of a confederate soldier, in fact, it was unlike any uniform Jacob had ever seen.

"How do I know what you say is true?" Jacob eased off the man's back.

"My badge. It's in my pocket." He jerked his head, indicating which pocket.

Holding both of the man's wrists with one hand, Jacob searched the pocket, pulling out a leather folder. Flipping it open, he read, "Officer George M. Walker. You are Officer Walker?"

The man cussed under his breath. "That's right."

Dashing to his feet, Jacob raised his hand to his forehead in salute. "My apologies, sir. I did not know you were an officer of the law. I thought you to be a Confederate soldier."

With surprising speed, the policeman was on his feet, his pistol out.

"Hands in the air. Turn around."

Jacob obeyed, turning slowly with arms upraised. He grimaced with pain but kept silent.

"Now, slowly, put your hands behind your back."

He did.

Officer Walker clicked cold metal cuffs in place over Jacob's wrists. He jerked him around so their faces were inches apart. Pain shot through Jacob's forearm.

"You are under arrest for assaulting a police officer. You have the—What's wrong with you?" Officer Walker stepped back, eyeing Jacob, "what's that on your shirt? Man! Is that blood?"

"Yes, sir," Jacob replied, "Nothing for which to be concerned. 'Tis naught but a flesh wound."

"A flesh wound? What kind of flesh wound?" The officer stepped closer, brows drawn, his lips turned down in a frown.

"I was shot, sir, just a grazing. Like I said, not a wound for which to be concerned."

"Not a wound for which to be concerned." The officer copied Jacob's accent, mocking his words. "And how did you get shot? Did you shoot yourself? The weapon still on you?"

Jacob rose to his full height and huffed with indignation as the officer patted him down, looking for his pistol. A pistol now safely contained in his satchel.

"Of course not, sir. I was shot by—" Jacob hesitated. It didn't seem right to tell the name of the man who shot him. As dreadful a person as Jethro could be, he probably never intended to actually shoot Jacob. Scare him into talking, yes, but shoot him? No. If Jacob hadn't rushed him to take back the journal, they would probably be sitting by the fire. The fire by the creek. Witch's Creek.

"—by a man at the creek."

"By the river you mean."

"Yes, sir."

"Well, I need to get you to the hospital and have that wound cleaned and cared for. We will return later to see if there's anyone down by the river."

"No need, I—"

"You want to go straight to jail?"

"No, sir."

"Then you go first to the hospital and get your arm checked."

"Yes, sir. Once again, my apologies—"

"And be quiet." Tossing the coat over Jacob's shoulder, Office Walker picked up the satchel, grasped Jacob by his good arm, and walked him down the gravel path to a black and white odd-shaped carriage parked along the road. It had thick black wheels with solid metal pokes filling the center. Glass panes covered the four sides.

Jacob stared. He had never seen a carriage such as this. Could this be one of those 'cars' Sofia mentioned in her journal?

Officer Walker leaned over, pulled a lever, and swung open a door, revealing a leather-cushioned seat.

"Get in." Walker gave Jacob a nudge toward the car.

Jacob crawled inside. His long legs touched the bench seat in front of him. A thick, clear glass with holes spaced intermittently separated his seat from the one in front. The officer leaned in, placing a strap over Jacob's shoulder and clicking it into place in a lock by his hip. Jacob watched every movement, fascinated.

"Are there really no horses to pull your carriage?" he asked.

Officer Walker burst out laughing, closing Jacob's door. He was still laughing when he opened the front door and sat behind a large wheel. Inserting a key, the officer turned it and the carriage emitted a low growl, then a steady rumble.

"This must be a car." Jacob tried to lean forward, but the strap locked his back to the bench seat. "I have never seen a car, much less ridden in one. I did read that they ride with unusual speed. May we go to the hospital at an unusual speed, Officer Walker?"

The officer shook his head, shoulders shaking with laughter. From the seat beside him, he lifted a pad of paper.

"Your name?"

"Jacob Reddington."

"Where do you live, Jacob Reddington?"

"St. Louis, Missouri."

"Birthdate?"

Jacob hesitated. Sofia had said to never tell her brother when he was from. It was probably not wise to tell the office either.

"March 12. I am twenty-five years old." There. He had answered without a lie.

"Huh. Twenty-five? You look older. Must be the mustache. Haven't seen one of those except in the movies."

Jacob fingered his handlebar mustache. He'd been proud of being able to grow it so thick. Many of the men in his unit couldn't do as well. Jacob studied the officer's cleanshaven face. Maybe mustaches weren't in fashion during this time. That would be a shame.

Putting the notebook down, Officer Walker turned the wheel, and the car began to move. Picking up speed, he drove down the dark street, lanterns beaming from the front of the car onto the road before them. As trees blurred past, Jacob leaned into the glass pane, his nose flattened against the cool surface. A broad smile spread across his face.

"Sir?" Jacob spoke up, not taking his eyes from the blur of trees and houses as they drove past. "May I ask what day this is?"

"Monday."

"What date?"

"June 2."

"Sorry, sir, I keep forgetting, I'm awful bad with numbers." So there went his first lie. "But can you remind me of the year?"

Officer Walker glanced up at the mirror reflecting Jacob's profile.

"You really need to get clean, Mr. Reddington. Drugs fry your brain. It's 2014."

Drugs? Yes, Jacob could understand what the officer was thinking. He himself had seen many a man whose mind was altered by laudanum and other concoctions the doctors gave to alleviate the pain. He would have to try to be more careful about his choice of words.

He could feel his grin grow even wider. Sofia had been telling the truth. What he thought impossible was not. He had fallen forward in time to the year 2014.

CHAPTER SIXTEEN

At the Hospital

HOSPITALS OF THE FUTURE looked nothing like those of his past. Instead of blankets spread on the floor or even rows of cots, there were separate cubicles with beds that rose with the push of a button. Jacob was fascinated, pushing the head of his bed up and down, over and over. The feet also could be raised, but not as fully as the head.

He could hear Officer Walker laughing with a nurse outside of his room.

Everything was clean: white sheets, white curtains, even white pillows. Bright lights were everywhere, not flickering candles or the steady light of a lamp, but glass domes that shone like the sun. He discovered one of the buttons on his bed could make the light above his head turn on and off like magic.

A nurse, wearing blue trousers and a shapeless top to match, came in for the third time. "Mr. Reddington, can I help you?"

He beamed at her. Everyone was so eager to assist him, they were all so kind. "No, ma'am. I am fine, thank you for asking yet again. I will call if I have a need."

"But you did call me. *Three times.*"

Jacob shook his head. "No, ma'am. You must have heard someone else. I am content with this amazing bed. It does so many things."

She frowned, unable to hide her irritation. "Are you pushing the call light?"

"This button turns on the lights, does that call you as well?"

"No, the button with the picture of the nurse." She noticed his blank expression then pointed at a button showing a circle with a hat. "That is the nurse call light. Every time you push it, it calls me."

Jacob stared at the controls, overwhelmed with admiration for this era. "My apologies, ma'am. I did not know."

He couldn't help but grin.

With a shake of her head, the nurse returned his smile.

"I don't know what you're on, Mr. Reddington, but it has you acting like a child. Now, try and behave yourself. The doctor will be in soon."

The doctor was an olive-skinned man with a heavy accent. Once more, Jacob struggled not to stare. This time was so different. After cleaning the wound using soft white squares of cloth and a clear liquid that stung like red ants biting, the doctor covered it with a bandage, taping it in place.

"You're right, it's not much more than a scrape. You're a lucky man. Most gunshots that walk into this place don't fare so well. I'll give you some antibiotics to make sure it doesn't get infected. Keep a bandage over it for a day or two and you should be fine."

Jacob nodded. What were antibiotics?

The nurse said they would discharge him as soon as his medicine came up from the pharmacy. He nodded again, turning back to the controls on his bed. He would be sorry to leave this hospital.

Suddenly, a black rectangle hanging from the wall came alive. People were inside it, talking to each other, seeming oblivious to Jacob's presence.

"Whoa!" He sat bolt upright on the bed. "What are you folks doing up there?" They didn't hear him, so he repeated himself, more loudly this time. Officer Walker poked his head through the doorway.

"What's going on?"

"Those people—" Jacob pointed at the box.

"You mean the TV?"

"TV?"

"Television, yeah. Listen here Custer, if you don't like the news, turn it off or change the channel." With a huff and roll of the eyes, he turned back to his hallway conversation. "I've half a mind to ask for a psychiatric evaluation."

"Why don't you?" The woman's voice answered.

"Nah. Not part of my job description. Besides, I need to get back to work, and he seems harmless enough."

"Didn't you say he attacked you?"

"Yeah, but he was easy to subdue. I had him turned and handcuffed in no time. The fool thought I was a Confederate soldier! Can you imagine? Probably high as a kite."

"Drug test won't be back until tomorrow," the nurse said.

"He can sleep in a cell as well as here. Maybe better, since there won't be buttons to play with."

They both laughed. Jacob felt his face get hot. He must really look foolish to these people. He needed to hide his enthusiasm, try to pretend that he was not surprised and amazed at every turn. His nurse came back into the room, eyeing the controls in Jacob's hands.

"Well, Mr. Reddington, your discharge is in order. Here's a paper with the doctor's instructions on cleaning your arm. Take these antibiotics, one tablet three times a day for seven days." She handed him a bottle with some tablets. "If you don't have any questions, sign here and you can go."

Questions? He had a million, beginning with these anty-bi-otics and those people in the TV box. He opened his mouth to ask, thought better of it and signed the paper.

The drive to the police station was as mesmerizing as the ride to the hospital. Officer Walker didn't bother to put the handcuffs on this time, and Jacob was grateful. Those things were not built for comfort. The car pulled in front of a red brick building and its hum came to a stop.

Led from the car, Jacob waited as Officer Walker unlocked the door. The darkness inside evaporated with a slide of the officer's hand against the wall. Instead of glass domes, the ceiling had long tubes that flickered like a fire trying to take hold, then came to full brightness, lighting up the whole room. Jacob stared. Would wonders never cease?

"Get your sorry self in here, Mr. Reddington," Officer Walker's voice had an impatient edge to it. He must be really peeved about being kept up so late into the night like this.

"I apologize once again, sir." Jacob felt bad about having knocked the man on the ground like he had, then causing all the inconvenience of taking him to the hospital. "I did not realize you were an officer of the law."

"Oh, sure. Tell me one more time who you thought I was." He laughed, his tone one of mocking.

"I thank you for taking me to the physician. I am much obliged."

"Save it, General Custer." The officer slapped a black square onto the top of the table. That was the second time he had called Jacob Custer. They looked nothing alike, aside from the mustache. He needed to clarify.

"Do you refer to Brigadier General Custer? I am not he, sir. I am Jacob Reddington, of St. Louis."

Officer Walker snickered, grasping Jacob's hands and pressing one finger at a time into the black ink pad, he then used the finger to make prints on a sheet of paper. Jacob watched, wondering what he was doing.

"We'll put this in the computer, and by tomorrow we'll know who you really are."

Jacob froze. Did they have the ability to identify a person simply by the marks of his fingers? What if they discovered Jacob was from a different time? What would they do with him then?

"Georgie," a woman's voice called from the dark corner of a locked cell, "you forgot to give him his phone call."

Phone call? Jacob's pulse increased. What was it the doctor said about the number she had him memorize? *"It's very important you don't share that number until you need it. You will know when that opportunity arrives. When you place the call, you are to remain where you are. My brother will send someone to get you. He'll do whatever it takes to help. My brother is a good man—not always safe, but good."*

She'd called it a telephone number. He felt a thrill. The doctor knew. She had known he was going to fall forward in time. The number, the letter, her journal. She had been preparing him all along.

"I can make a phone call?" Jacob could barely contain his excitement. He had no idea what it meant, but he was actually completing the task the lady doctor sent him to do. "On a telephone?"

"Well you sure ain't gonna make it from something else." Officer Walker glared in the direction of the cell. He didn't appear to appreciate the woman telling him how to do his job.

"I would like to make a phone call. On the telephone, please. I know a number to call." Jacob tried to look relaxed, like this was something he'd done a hundred times before. It didn't work. The officer pursed his lips, his fingers making a circle near his temples in the age-old symbol indicating someone was not all right in the head.

"Phone is right there." He pointed to a bulky black device on the desk.

Jacob stared down at it, lifted the receiver and inspected it, turning it over in his hand, then put it down again. Did he need to speak to it? Or rub it like Aladdin and the genie in the bottle?

"Sir, would you be so kind as to instruct me on its use?"

The officer sneered. Lifting the handpiece and handing it back to Jacob. "Okay, Custer. You speak in this end, listen on the other. Think you got that?"

"I speak into this device, and the person hears me in their own location?" It was amazing. Everything was so amazing.

Officer Walker rolled his eyes. "Here, give me the number. I'll punch it in for you."

Jacob hesitated. The doctor had said not to share the number until he needed it. Well, this qualified as a need-it moment. He rattled off the number, holding the receiver to his ear. After a series of tones he could hear ringing, then a voice. "Leave a message at the beep." Then a long beep and silence. He looked up at the officer, "It says, leave a message at the beep."

It's your one phone call." Officer Walker shrugged. "Use it or lose it."

Jacob nodded. "My name is Jacob Reddington and I am...Where am I again, sir?"

"Monroe County Jail."

"I am at the Monroe County Jail. I have a letter for you from your sister." He waited. There was another beep. No one answered.

"There is no reply," he said, looking at the officer, wondering what he had done wrong. "Are you sure he can hear me?"

"You got voicemail." The officer took the receiver from Jacob and put it back on its base. "That's your one phone call. Time to lock you up."

"Come on, Georgie." The woman's voice again. She must be held in this place frequently to be on a first name basis with the officer. "Help the guy out. Jacob, you should ask for a lawyer."

"That will not be necessary." Jacob turned to look in her direction. The lights back there were dim, but he could make out that she was a slight thing, barely larger than a child, bundled up in a blanket. "The woman who gave me the telephone number said I should wait. Her brother will assist me."

Another snicker from the officer. Jacob wondered if he would ever fit in.

There were two cells at the back of the large room, not unlike those of his own time. Thick metal bars rose from ceiling to floor, and similar bars separated the cells in the middle. Officer Walker opened the empty cell and motioned Jacob inside. He went without complaint, thankful that he would not be spending the night on the hard cement bench.

He wondered if Jethro still lay unconscious by the river. Officer Walker said a park ranger went to investigate, so

Jacob decided it was no longer his concern. Jethro could fend for himself.

"Watch out for the girl next to you. She's meaner than she looks." Officer Walker closed the door and turned the key. Taking Jacob's bag, he opened a safe and put it inside. Grabbing a blanket from a shelf, he tossed it through the bars. Jacob caught it with his uninjured arm.

"You two have a pleasant night. We'll be back to check on you in a few hours. And," he nodded at a small box on the ceiling, "in case you try anything, we got you on camera."

Jacob sat on the bench, watching the officer grab his coat and head out the front door. With a swipe of his hand across the wall by the door, the room went dark.

Amazing. It was all amazing.

He rubbed his hand across his forehead. Tomorrow, Sofia's brother, Chachi, would come. Jacob tried to imagine what he was like. Having not seen his sister for many years, Chachi would be full of questions Jacob could not answer. What was it she had said? *My brother is a good man—not always safe, but good.*

CHAPTER SEVENTEEN

The Girl From His Dreams

"You should have asked for a lawyer." The woman spoke, startling Jacob from his wonderings.

Goodness, what was he thinking? He leaped to his feet.

Dim light from a streetlamp outside lit the desks but left the back of the room in shadows.

"I beg your pardon, miss, I forgot my manners." He went to lift his hat in greeting, feeling foolish as he gripped nothing but air. Somewhere in the deep past, a hat sat perched on a branch, waving in the wind and waiting for some passerby to find it. They would wonder at the deserted shelter and supplies, but not in their wildest dreams could they figure out what happened.

Jacob squinted, trying to see the girl better. She looked familiar.

"I am sorry, miss, but have we met?" As soon as the question was asked, Jacob realized how foolish it was. Of course they had never met.

"Oh, brother. Not that line." She pulled her blanket closer around her shoulders. "I don't think so, General Custer."

That Custer thing again. What was it about these people? He needed to disabuse her of that notion.

"Why do people keep calling me that? I am not General Custer." Jacob reached through the bars, extending his hand in greeting. "Name is Jacob. Jacob Reddington."

He couldn't get over the feeling that he knew this woman. Did she remind him of someone? If he could only get a closer look, maybe he could tell why. "Are you sure we are not acquainted?"

"Not in this life." Her answer sent a chill down his spine. She fully extended her arm and gave Jacob's hand a brief but firm shake. Her fingers were cold. She pulled back and tucked her arm back under the warmth of her blanket. Jacob noticed a slight shiver.

"You are cold." Jacob grasped the blanket Officer Walker had tossed his way and held it toward her. "Please, take my blanket. I have a coat. It will suffice."

She turned her head as though studying him before slipping from her covers and rising. She didn't take her eyes from his as she stepped toward him.

Jacob's heart skipped a beat. It couldn't be, but he knew those eyes, that face. He felt his knees weaken, and he swallowed hard and handed her the blanket. His hand trembled as her fingers brushed his.

"It is you." His voice was but a whisper, his heart rose to his throat. She was real. The girl of his dreams, she stood in front of him in flesh and blood.

Her eyes narrowed, and she raised one side of her lip in distaste. "Yeah, it's me, and I don't know you. Stop staring. You don't look so good yourself."

Jacob felt the rush of blood into his cheeks. He must look like a total fool.

The young woman turned, swirling the blanket up and over her shoulders, then glanced back in his direction as she returned to her bench. "What happened to your shoulder?"

"I was shot," Jacob said. He needed to figure out a way to get her to talk, but what do you say to the woman of your dreams?

"Seriously? So how exactly did you go about getting shot?"

Jacob sighed. He didn't want to talk about Jethro, didn't want to remember their last encounter, or any of their previous ones, for that matter. He could see Jethro standing at the creek's edge, holding out the doctor's journal above the water. "Let us just say someone I used to work with tried to take something very precious to me."

"Did you get it back?"

"Yes." Jacob watched as she lay down, spreading the blankets, one atop the other, over her slim figure. An overwhelming sense of appreciation filled him for Jethro's foolhardy behavior. If it hadn't been for that man's meddling, Jacob would not be here today, in the same room with this beautiful woman.

"Well, I hope it was worth it," she said.

"Yes. It was worth more than I knew."

He stared, half dazed. He had to stop it. The girl clearly thought he was annoying.

"You in a gang?" she asked.

Missouri was full of roving gangs, like the one that had attacked their unit, the one that killed Johnny. Jacob felt his fists tighten. He could never be part of the lawless predators like them. Was that what she thought of him? He forced his fists to relax. Was he any better? His war crimes would haunt him until the day he died.

She waited, looking at him from the corner of her eye like she knew the answer.

"No, miss." Jacob hesitated. How much should he explain? "I was in the war."

Pity filled her dark eyes. He could see it, even through the shadows of the room. "Oh, that explains it. What'd you do? To get arrested?"

Heat rushed to his face again. He stared down at his feet. What could he say that didn't make him look so foolish? He finally got to meet the woman he'd been dreaming of, and she thought him a gang member. Someone to be pitied.

"I was asleep on a bench. The lawman awoke me. I thought he was a Confederate soldier, and I wrestled him to the ground."

Her laugh was like music, clear and unexpected. Apparently it surprised her as well, since she brought the blanket up to stifle its sound. He wanted to tell her not to worry, to keep laughing. The sound of it was the most beautiful thing he had heard in—well, his whole life.

"Confederates. Wow. Keep telling people that, and you'll get yourself committed to the mental hospital."

Mrs. Powers had said as much. Jacob felt himself grinning as he stretched out on the bench. He lay still, listening to the sounds of her breathing. It was a dream. It had to be. The girl was real.

"Pardon my intrusion, miss," Jacob raised his head and peered through the bars. "I did not get your name."

"Anna Marie Johnson. And no, we haven't met."

Warmth spread through him as if he was sitting in front of a fire on a cold evening. He rolled her name over and over in his mind. Anna Marie Johnson. It suited her.

"Of course, you are right. We have not met until now." His smile grew bigger, he couldn't hold it back. If she only knew. "It is a pleasure meeting you, Miss Johnson."

She huffed and turned on her side. "Stop calling me 'Miss.' It's Anna Marie. Just Anna Marie."

A chill spread across Jacob's chest, and his breath caught in his throat. Not 'Miss'? He lurched upright, almost falling off the narrow bench that doubled as a bed. "You are married?"

"No, I'm not married. It's just weird—you calling me 'Miss.' It's like I'm at a job interview or something."

Jacob sighed, the warmth filling his chest once more, and he relaxed back onto his bench. He felt the smile spread across his face, and he made no effort to stop it. She was real, and she was unmarried.

"What did *you* do, Just Anna Marie Johnson, to find yourself detained in jail?"

"Stabbed the Sergeant."

She spoke so matter-of-factly that Jacob thought he misheard.

"What?"

"With a letter opener. He wouldn't listen to me."

"Tell me. What occurred to cause you to react so?"

He could picture it. This tiny little lady was big in spirit. He'd seen it in her since his first dream. When she began to speak, her voice was hesitant at first then picked up courage. It was as though once she began to tell her story, she couldn't stop. Jacob leaned his head in her direction, not wanting to miss a word she said.

Her story broke his heart. A girl, abandoned first by her mother, then her father. Raised by an elderly aunt and holding tight to her identical twin sister.

He could feel her desperation when she spoke of her sister going missing. It explained so much of what he saw of her over the last few months. His dreams—understanding dawned on Jacob—those visions of Anna Marie had been of times when her emotions were at their highest. Somehow, in her loneliness, she had reached to him across time. He had been helpless to help her then. Maybe now…

"I saw her reflection in my mirror, like a million pieces of myself in the water droplets. When they evaporated, she was gone."

She glanced nervously at Jacob, as though wondering how he would respond. His mouth went dry. In the water droplets? Like the reflection he had seen of Anna Marie in the creek? Could her sister be back in time? Or forward?

Jacob blinked, nodding at Anna Marie to continue. He listened. When she spoke of hearing her sister's song, he nodded.

She sighed, a nervous shudder to her breath like she had been holding it for a long, long time.

Jacob shook his head in wonder. How could he explain to her that he understood and believed her?

"The world does not always work the way we think it should. I have seen things I never thought possible and are likely inexplicable. I do not believe you are delusional, Just Anna Marie."

He hesitated, afraid to say more. Would she think he was insane? Mulling over possible responses, he closed his eyes. Truth was, he had no idea what the right thing to say would be. He had no idea what was possible in this time. If they could make lights turn off and on and hold people in little boxes called televisions, was time travel a routine part of life? He didn't think so. Not from the reaction the lawman had given him. Yet, he had to try.

"What if—what if your sister is trying to communicate with you? Not just from some *where* else, but from some *when* else?"

She snorted and glared at him. "Yeah, right, General Custer. Like time travel is a thing. You'd have to be deranged to believe that."

All right. So, no. Don't bring up the time travel theory again. That didn't go over so well. Jacob lay still, thinking. His thoughts turned to prayers.

Lord, my being here is Your doing. There is no other explanation. Her being here is Your doing as well. Thank You for that. Help me to know what to say and do so as not to drive her away from me.

Her breathing deepened. Jacob studied her petite form, wondering what the rest of her story was. What made her happy? How did she pass her days? With both parents and her aunt gone, who watched over her? Would he ever be able to share his story with her? Tell her where he came from?

"It's true, Just Anna Marie," he whispered, not wanting to awaken her but needing to tell her nonetheless. "It happened to me. I traveled near one hundred fifty years. I came through water."

Jacob pulled his coat up over his shoulders, watching this girl from his dreams as she slept not twenty feet from him. He would never understand God's doings, but here he was, in a time and place that should not contain him. With her.

Even in her sleep, the pull of her brows carried a heavy sadness. The way her lips pursed reminded him of a little child who was frightened and alone.

The song rose in his memory, and Jacob began to hum. As the melody filled the room, he watched. Anna Marie's brow relaxed, and bit by bit, her lips lengthened into a gentle smile.

The End (for now.)

NOTE FROM THE AUTHOR

Hi! I'm Brenda, and I want to thank you for reading Jacob's story. My first book, Anna's Song: Cries From the Earth, Book 1, tells the story of Anna Marie and her search for her missing sister, beginning just before her encounter with Jacob in jail. Sofia's Beauty: Cries From the Earth Book 2, is the story behind the mysterious lady doctor Jacob knows as Mrs. Powers. This, Jacob's story, bridges the two.

Will Jacob win Anna Marie's heart? Where will this dream lead him, and what price is he willing to pay to keep Anna Marie safe?

If you enjoyed this novella, please leave a review on Amazon and Good Reads so that other readers like you can discover these books. For new authors, word of mouth and reviews are how our works get known. Thank you!

Read on for the first Chapter of Anna's Song.

ANNA'S SONG

CHAPTER ONE

Mirror, Mirror

BEFORE I fell through the water, I thought I was crazy. "Hey, doc, you know that sister of mine everyone presumes dead? She's alive just like I said. Yes, sir. Saw her yesterday, in my bathroom mirror."

"Of course, you will 'see' Adeline in the mirror," my imaginary psychiatrist replies, chuckling like it's some private joke. "After all, you do look alike."

Adeline is my twin sister. Identical in every way except for a birthmark, a scar, and some serious leg muscles.

I run when I'm upset, and I've been running a lot. You see, ten months, eleven days, and somewhere between twelve and sixteen hours ago, Adeline disappeared.

The first time I saw my missing sister, I had just gotten out of the shower, and the mirror was all misty.

Opening the door to let some of the extra moisture dissipate, I glanced up, and there she was, staring back at me through the myriad droplets on the glass. For a moment, I thought it was my own reflection, but her hair was dry, and, suffice it to say, we weren't exactly in the same state of dress. She looked as astonished as I felt, and when the mirror cleared, she was gone.

With my heart pounding something awful, I staggered to my room and collapsed on the edge of my bed, forcing myself to take slow, deep breaths and thinking I had seen a ghost. But she was no ghost. You can't be a ghost if you're still among the living.

People keep saying she's dead. I know better.

There's this thing about twins. We know stuff about each other in ways most singletons can't comprehend. Adeline and I never feel each other's pain. When she broke her arm, mine felt fine. When my appendix ruptured, she didn't writhe in bed. We don't read each other's thoughts, but we often perceive what the other is thinking. We aren't much alike, outside of appearances.

Still, I can always tell my sister *is*, in the same way I know I *am*. I can sense her heart beating as sure as I sense my own. I feel her soul the same way the first violinist can feel the music playing around her. We gave up trying to explain this to people. It's like pointing out a complex harmony to someone who is tone deaf. I hear her in my very bones.

The next morning, there in the mist of the mirror, she stands. I blink hard, trying to keep myself calm, and raise my right hand in a stiff wave.

"It's just me," I whisper to the image in front of me. Maybe, if I say it enough, my imagination will back off. "It's just my reflection."

She raises her right hand. Her right, not the mirror image of mine, and wiggles her fingers in a tentative wave. I open the door and run. Determined to never look in the mirror again, I ignore the crushing tension in my chest, squeezing me until I want to weep, or scream, or both. Instead, I go about singing at the top of my lungs until the neighbor's dog yowls in protest, and all crawly creatures evacuate the region. Okay, I exaggerate. I do that a lot.

Then I run like twenty times around the block.

Three days pass, and my nails are nubbins. The neighbors are complaining, and I do what any sane person does to relax. Take a bath. A nice, long, hot bath. It works. It works so well I forget not to look in the mirror when I get out.

There she is, looking down at me like she's looking down a well. Her hair is pulled back tight against her scalp and into a bun. What? Adeline isn't vain, but this is beyond even her lack of style. The phantom image laughs and lifts up a newspaper. The paper's name, underlined three times, catches my eye. It's not one I'm familiar with. In the corner, the date is circled. Beneath the two, penned in my sister's meticulous handwriting, is a message. I lean in closer, rub my eyes, and read it again.

This can't be real.

She shrugs and fades along with the tiny droplets, leaving me in stunned silence.

Standing there like someone super glued my feet to the floor, I stare at the mirror. My true reflection is all that remains, eyes large, gripped with the fear of seeing "her" again, and terrified that I may not.

The harsh jangle of the phone jerks me back to the present. No one calls me except for telemarketers and political fundraisers. I let the answering machine respond.

"Hi! You've reached the Johnson sisters. Please leave a message." Adeline's voice echoes through the room, a voice that once filled every day of my life.

I will never change that recording.

"Miss Johnson, this is Sergeant Bowman. Could you—"

I grab at the phone before he can hang up. "Yes, this is Anna Marie. Any news?"

"No. I'm sorry." The voice on the other end hesitates. "Anna Marie? Could you come by the office? Perhaps in the morning? We need to discuss a few things."

"I'll be right over." I hang up before he has a chance to protest. Already I'm pulling on a pair of jeans. Grabbing the first T-shirt I find, I wiggle it over my head and rush out the door. My flip-flops thump, thump, thump as I run across the front porch, down the stairs, and to my car.

Adeline. She's out there somewhere. I have to find her.

I park in front of the handicap sign—it's the only vacant spot close to the front door of our diminutive police department. Inside, Officer Walker glances up and clears his throat. Not making eye contact, he busies himself rearranging files in the cabinet. Sergeant Bowman is at his desk, and by the slump of his shoulders I know I will not appreciate what he has to say.

Coldness grips my stomach. I clench my fists and march to the chair in front of his desk where I've sat on so many visits before. I notice my shirt is inside out. Doesn't matter. Nerves make my legs tingle and burn as they bounce in agitated excitement. An overwhelming urge to run hits me, but I don't. I need to know what he knows.

Three folders are laid out on the desk in front of him. Adeline's is open, pages dog-eared and worn. Her high school graduation picture, a staple puncturing top and bottom, smiles from the upper left corner. Adeline Johnson, age 18, DOB 1/31/1995. Missing 8/21/2013. Every report, every picture inside is burned deep into my memory.

The other two folders sit alongside my sister's. I glance at them, then look away. My heart is cold as stone. These belong to our parents. They left us, and I'm to blame.

Sofia Johnson, age 27,
DOB 9/27/1974 Missing 9/11/2001.
Case unresolved.

Roger Johnson, age 34,
DOB 12/10/1968. Missing 10/12/2002.
Case unresolved.

We were seven when Mama left, eight when our father followed suit.

"Thank you for coming." Sergeant Bowman pulls at his collar and glances up at the clock like he wishes he were anywhere but here.

Our eyes lock for a brief moment before he looks away.

"I wish I had better news. You know I spent hours on your sister's case, particularly in light of similar reports about your parents." He closes Adeline's folder, rests his hands, palms down, over the top. His little finger is blocking her face.

I want to reach over and move his hand.

"The fact is, we have no clues about what happened to your sister. The more time that passes, the less likely we are to find any. The case is cold, Anna, and I can't in good conscience spend more tax dollars without a lead."

I'm shaking my head. *No. No. Please.* Ringing echoes in my ears, and I compel myself to breathe. I stare at his Adam's apple. It slides down below the rim of his collar and up again as he swallows. Behind us, the drawer on a file cabinet slams shut.

"I'm sorry, Hon." The Sergeant rearranges his collar once more. "The department is calling off the investigation."

I blink, my vision narrowing.

"You can't do this." My voice breaks.

This man knows my sister. We went to school with his children. He always bought way more Girl Scout cookies from us than any two-man police department could eat. How can he give up?

"You don't understand. She's out there!"

I'm standing now. "Sir, I've borrowed against the house. Every penny I make goes to searching for Adeline. I have nothing left. You gotta help me find her!"

"Anna Marie, she likely drowned. You know that. The underground caves, perhaps. No one knows, but her body—"

"No!" Tears will not flow. Crying is for the weak. I see nothing but my anger, my frustration. Why doesn't anyone understand? Adeline is every bit alive as I am. She needs me. I have to make him listen.

It's not my fault the Sergeant has a real letter opener out on his desk. I mean, really, someone who deals with criminals for a living should know better, even if we live in Po-dunk, Missouri where nothing ever happens. Except to my family. When my vision clears, we both stare at the wavering letter opener embedded deep into the wood of the desk. Blood oozes from the webbing between the Sergeant's thumb and forefinger where I nicked it.

Uh-oh.

Strong hands grab me. Officer Walker is twisting my arms behind me, pulling me away. I struggle, kicking, writhing, trying to get free.

"No!" I moan, my knees giving way as my energy evaporates into despair. "Please. She's alive. I still feel her."

Made in the USA
Columbia, SC
11 July 2025